THE SILVER TOWER

RISE OF THE KING
BOOK TWO

TJ GREEN

The Silver Tower
Published by Mountolive Publishing
©2020 TJ Green
1st Edition2017 TJ Green
All rights reserved
ISBN 978-1-99-004701-5

Cover Design by Fiona Jayde Media
Editing by Sue Copsey and Missed Period Editing

To Lawrence Durrell, my first love

And every marge enclosing in the midst
A square of text that looks a little blot,
The text no larger than the limbs of fleas;
And every square of text an awful charm,
Writ in a language that has long gone by.

– Alfred, Lord Tennyson (1809–92)

Titles available by TJ Green

Rise of the King Series
Call of the King
The Silver Tower
The Cursed Sword

White Haven Witches Series
Buried Magic
Magic Unbound
Magic Unleashed
All Hallows' Magic
Undying Magic
Crossroads Magic
Crown of Magic

White Haven Hunters
Spirit of the Fallen

Invite from the author -

If you'd like to read more about Tom, you can get two free short stories, *Excalibur Rises* and *Jack's Encounter*, by subscribing to my newsletter.
By staying on my mailing list you'll receive free excerpts of my new books, as well as short stories, news of giveaways, and a chance to join my launch team. I'll also be sharing information about other books in this genre you might enjoy.
To get your FREE book and short story please visit my website - http://www.tjgreen.nz
I look forward to you joining my readers' group.

Chapter 1 Vivian's Request

Tom leaned on the parapet that edged the throne room of the Aerie and looked across the vast expanse of Aeriken Forest, thinking how different it was now from when he had first visited so many months ago.

The air of brooding intensity and fear was gone, and now the whole place rustled with life and vitality. He could feel it, even so far above the canopy. The Aerie, the palace where they had battled Queen Gavina, otherwise known as Morgan le Fay, had been transformed, too.

A few weeks earlier, Tom had returned with his cousin, Beansprout, to visit Brenna, their bird-shifter friend and heir to the throne, and to help with some palace repairs. Now, it was virtually complete. He turned his back on the forest views to look at the room behind him.

The throne room had severe black granite walls, tall columns that stretched to the open sky above, and shallow pools of water that rippled in the breeze, but everything looked different from that fateful night.

They had swept away the shale and flint that had slipped from the walls, and the throne was back in its proper spot after Prince Finnlugh had magically dragged it across the floor. Huge swags of branches and leaves now hung from the walls and columns, brightening everything, and an air of hope filled the air.

The copper-embellished doors swung open at the far end, and Beansprout stuck her head inside. "Here you are! I've been looking for you!" She crossed the space to join him. "You like it in here, don't you?"

Beansprout, like him, had decided to stay in the Otherworld. It suited her here, he realised. Her long, strawberry blonde hair shimmered in the sunlight, and she glowed with health. It sounded silly, but Tom couldn't think of a better way to describe it.

He smiled at her. "I do. I love the view. And I love the fact that this place looks so different now, since Morgan has gone."

"It feels good, doesn't it?" she said, leaning on the parapet next to him. "I like that we made a difference."

"What now, though? It's finished. The Aeriken don't need our help anymore."

"True. We could head back to Vanishing Hall and see Granddad."

"I'm not sure Arthur's there. He was going to see Vivian," Tom reminded her.

"I think Woodsmoke went, too," Beansprout said thoughtfully. "But that's okay, they'll be back."

Vanishing Hall was their fey friend, Woodsmoke's, ancestral home. He lived there with his father, who barely ventured from his tower, his grandfather, Fahey, who was a bard, and now Tom and Beansprout's granddad, Jack.

She continued to speak, her gaze distant as she surveyed the forest. "I think we should venture beyond the village when we get back, see some more of this world!"

"Maybe see Finnlugh!" Tom suggested, feeling excited. Prince Finnlugh, Head of the House of Evernight, and Bringer of Starfall and Chaos, had helped them defeat

Morgan, and had welcomed them to his Under-Palace for a visit. "I miss him. And it would be good to see his palace when it's not stuffed full of sprites." He shuddered remembering his encounter there, when he'd rescued Brenna.

"Yes, let's! And we can travel back home without an escort, too. That will be fun."

The Aerikeen had spent the proceeding weeks opening up all the paths across the forest, and hunting down the final sprites that still lurked in the furthest reaches of Aeriken. Tom had helped them clear the main path to Vanishing Wood, and now felt reasonably confident to travel without getting lost. Where the paths had branched, signs had been placed, too. Although the trip would take a few days, it was now perfectly safe to travel alone, and Tom secretly enjoyed their independence from everyone, and he knew Beansprout did, too.

Before he could answer, there was a whirr of wings above them, and a black bird swooped into the hall, transforming before their eyes into Brenna. "You too look like you're up to something!" she said, a glint in her eye.

"It doesn't matter how many times I see you do that," Tom said, "it's still amazing."

"I wish you could do it, too. It's the best feeling in the world!" She narrowed her eyes at them. "But you haven't answered the question! What are you plotting?"

"Not plotting," Beansprout said, laughing. "Planning what we do next. You don't need us anymore, so we thought we'd go home."

"Interesting you should say that," Brenna said, smoothing down the tiny feathers that edged her hairline. Now she didn't have to disguise herself, she looked like the other bird-shifters. Feathers threaded thickly though her long hair and edged her forehead, her eyes had become darker, and her eyebrows more pronounced. She looked, Tom had to admit, seriously hot, and he tried to push those thoughts to the back of his mind. She continued, "We've just received a message from Woodsmoke and Arthur."

"Have we? How?" Beansprout asked.

"By bird, idiot," Tom answered.

Beansprout glared at him. "I'm not an idiot."

"Well, we haven't got telephones anymore!" he pointed out. Or TV, or cars, or radio, or any electronic anything, and Tom didn't miss them one bit.

Brenna swiftly intervened. "Private bird message. Woodsmoke used a carrier pigeon from Vanishing Village. They're travelling on to Holloways Meet, and they've asked us to join them. Shall I say yes?"

"Yes!" Tom said immediately. "What's Holloways Meet?"

"It's a place where all of the Holloways converge, making a small town. It's a hub for all sorts of news. You'll like it."

"And the Holloways are?"

"Sunken lanes that cross this part of the Otherworld. You'll see. Beansprout, do you want to come?"

"Of course!"

"We'll need more supplies than we have here, so we'll stop by the village, too. We'll be a few days behind them, but that's okay. Woodsmoke said he'll leave another message there just in case there's a change of meeting place, but that's the plan for now. We won't have time to stop and see Jack and Fahey, though."

Tom sat on the huge throne, and threw his legs over the side arm. "But why are we going? It sounds like we have to rush."

"Our special friend Vivian has asked for Arthur's help. One of her priestesses called Nimue has disappeared, and she's worried about her. Arthur has agreed to find her. I don't know the details, but yes, we need to leave today."

She was referring to Vivian, the Lady of the Lake, who had summoned Tom to the Otherworld all those months ago. But Nimue? "Who? Oh, wait. I think I know that name." Tom had always read lots about King Arthur, and he remembered that she was one of the famous women in the tales.

"She lives on Avalon, too, apparently," Brenna said.

Tom nodded. "Yes, she had some sort of love affair with Merlin, I think." He could hardly believe that these people had really existed. That some still existed. "But I didn't see anyone else on Avalon."

"She probably remained in the temple buildings while you were there. Anyway, she's gone and could be in trouble, so she's asked Arthur to find her. We'll find out more when we join them. As it's still early, I thought we could leave today."

Beansprout looked at Brenna, arms across her chest. "Shouldn't you really be staying here?"

Brenna's guilty look swiftly disappeared. "No! I have done what I promised to do. The Aerie is clean, the paths are open, and the dead are buried."

Tom groaned, knowing exactly what Beansprout was getting at. "But you're their Queen!"

"Don't you start with that. I'm not. I haven't agreed to be, and I'm not sure I'm going to." Brenna held her hand up

11

in a stop sign. "No! I will not discuss this now. I need to get out. This is the perfect opportunity!" She dropped her voice, and it became a plea. "I need this. They keep asking me about when I'm going to have my coronation. It's driving me insane!"

"Who'll lead them when you're gone?" Tom asked.

"I'll ask my cousin, Orel. He's competent, smart, and everyone likes him. And most importantly, he's trustworthy."

Tom nodded, knowing who she meant. He'd spoken with him a few times over the last few weeks. "That's a good choice."

"Exactly. Can you be packed in an hour? No, say two, so I can say my goodbyes and reassure everyone."

Tom leapt to his feet, as Beansprout started walking to the door. "Yep! Saddle the horses!"

"See you in the stables, then!" And Brenna quickly changed form and plunged over the parapet to the stables below to organise their departure.

They had been travelling through the quiet of the forest for days, so it was a shock to emerge into bright sunshine. The light bouncing off the river dazzled Tom and he blinked, holding a hand across his eyes to shield them from the sun that was high overhead. On the opposite bank, he could see Vanishing Village and the high bridges and walkways that spanned the buildings.

He grinned at the sight. It had been weeks since he'd been there. How could he have ever doubted that being in the Otherworld was the single greatest gift of his life? Everything here seemed to have an intensity he hadn't noticed before. The air was perfumed with a delicate blossom and honey scent, and the colours seemed bright and sharp with a richness that his Earth didn't seem to have. He could hear bees buzzing and birds singing, and the sounds of fey from the village drifted across the river with a clarity that startled him.

"You all right, Tom?" Beansprout asked, smiling.

"Absolutely," he said, unable to stop smiling. "I forgot how much Otherworld villages are so different from our own. I'm glad I stayed. I'm glad you helped me make the right decision."

Beansprout hugged him unexpectedly. "I'm glad you stayed, too. Although I think it was Arthur more than me who made you see sense." She turned to look over at the village and threw her arms wide. "This place feels full of possibilities, and it's so odd, but so cool at the same time! I love it!"

"For the record, I'm glad you stayed, too," Brenna said looking fondly at both of them. "But I'm afraid we haven't got time to linger. I've organised supplies, so once we've picked them up, we'll push on."

They threaded through the narrow streets of the village, surrounded by the bustle of fey of all different shapes and sizes. Tom would have loved to be able to look around the place for a little longer, but after packing their saddle bags with supplies, Brenna picked up Woodsmoke's latest message from the pigeon carriers on the edge of the village, and scanned it quickly.

"There's no change in the plan, so we're still to go to the Meet. They've stopped at another couple of villages to ask questions, but no one remembers Nimue, and he's asked us to ask anyone we see, too," she shrugged. "Just in case. Let's go."

They headed along a road that led in the opposite direction from Avalon, towards the rolling hills in the distance. Over to the right was the river Tom had travelled along in Fews's boat on his first visit, and beyond that was Prince Finnlugh's labyrinthine House of Evernight.

It was a road unlike any Tom had been on before. Before long, it had burrowed into the surrounding fields, becoming rutted and worn. High banks topped by hedgerows shielded them from view, and trees arched above them, plunging them into a green and shadowy place. It smelt of pollen-soaked earthiness and it was quiet, the horses' hooves muffled by the dusty path.

"What's so special about the Meet?" Tom asked, shuffling on his horse, Midnight, trying to find his rhythm. He still wasn't comfortable riding, despite the fact that he'd had a lot more practice.

Brenna, effortlessly graceful astride her horse next to him, said, "Woodsmoke said it's the last place Vivian knew Nimue had been."

"What was she doing there?"

"I think it was just a place to stop on the way to Dragon's Hollow, where she was going to meet the sorcerer, Raghnall. She would have probably restocked for her journey there."

"How long will it take us to get there?"

"A few days. We just keep following this road and we'll get there eventually. We're on one of the old Holloways now. Some people call them the hidden ways. They run all across the Otherworld like warrens between places."

"It's like travelling in secret," Beansprout said, lit up by the pale rays of sunshine breaking through the leaf cover.

"Except they're not a secret, not really," Brenna explained. "They're used by all sorts of creatures. I'm sure we'll meet a few as we travel. These paths were mostly formed by the Royal Houses as they moved back and forth between the various Under-Palaces."

"So we'll pass other Under-Palaces?" Tom asked.

"We'll pass close by. But don't get too excited. We probably won't see anyone from them. And you would never know if we passed by an entrance, because they would be disguised as part of the landscape." She gestured at the bank, covered in grasses and flowers. "That could be one. How would we know? Anyway, we'd better pick up the pace," she said, urging her horse to a trot, and Tom and Beansprout hurried to keep up.

They travelled for the rest of the day, breaking only for a brief rest mid-afternoon by a stream where the horses could drink. Every now and again they passed steep paths that led up to the fields around them, and eventually, as the sun began to set and the Holloway filled with billowing clouds of midges, Brenna led them up one of these paths and onto the meadows above them.

They gathered some dry wood and made a fire, preparing to camp for the night, and Tom watched Brenna preparing her bow to hunt.

"You know," Tom said warily, looking at Brenna, "that you do need to make a decision on your future at some point."

She groaned. "I'm trying to forget it for now! And anyway, why do you care?"

"Because you're my friend, and I think you'd be good at being a Queen! You helped me make the biggest decision of my life!"

"I'm aiming to put my decision off for as long as possible. I feel very guilty for having left them in the first place to go into hiding, so I don't feel I deserve it now."

"You were in fear of losing your life!" Beansprout reminded her.

"So were many others."

"Not like you. Morgan killed your parents."

"She killed a lot more than that in the end," she said, shaking her head with sorrow. "And I like travelling around with my friends, and I don't want to think I'll be shut up in the Aerie all day, making boring decisions."

"But if you're Queen, surely you can choose to rule however you want?" Tom suggested.

"There are still responsibilities. Things I will be expected to do."

"It didn't seem to stop Arthur when he ruled. He travelled, led battles, went everywhere he wanted... Well, if what I've read is true. There are so many stories. It's hard to know what was real and what was made up. If anyone can give advice on leadership, it's Arthur. You should ask him."

Chapter 2 The Hollow Bole

Tom and the others rode into Holloways Meet on a hot, dusty afternoon.

The road broadened and dipped until they reached a large archway formed by thick, interlaced branches. Beyond that, a few small buildings began to appear, built into the high banks of the road. Within a short distance they could hear a steady hum of voices, shouts, laughter, and music, and the banks fell back to form a large, irregular town square dominated by a central group of trees with other Holloways leading into it. It was filled with an assorted collection of beings, young and old, colourful and drab, and the smell of business.

Wooden buildings threaded through the meeting place, some of them perched precariously in branches, others jostling for position on the fields above them, casting deep shadows onto the activities in the centre.

"This place looks busier than ever," Brenna murmured.

"What do people do here?" Tom asked, looking around curiously.

"Many things. I have been told you can buy almost anything here. Consequently, a lot of people pass through, so it's particularly useful for finding out information."

"I love it!" Beansprout declared, her eyes darting everywhere.

"We'd better find Woodsmoke and Arthur. Woodsmoke said he would try to check into the Quarter Way House," Brenna told them, and pointed to a big building with balconies on the far side of the square, built against the bank and onto the field at the top. "It's more expensive than most inns, but it guarantees a clean bed and good food."

They found Woodsmoke and Arthur sitting in a bar to the side of the main entrance. It was an oasis of calm after the bustle of the square, filled with an assortment of tables and chairs, and screened from the square by thick-limbed climbing plants covered with flowers and a coating of wind-blown dust.

"Well, don't you two look relaxed!" Brenna said, hands on hips.

"The rest of the deserving after a hard day's work!" Woodsmoke smirked as he and Arthur stood to greet them. "Tom—you've grown." He walked around the table and grabbed him in a bear hug, before hugging Beansprout and Brenna. "I've missed you two, too. Look at you, Brenna!" He held her at arm's length, taking in her hair.

"Woodsmoke, it's only been a few weeks since I last saw you," Brenna said, protesting weakly.

"I don't care. It's good to see you looking like a bird-shifter again!"

Tom had forgotten it had been a while since Woodsmoke had seen Brenna, but he was distracted by Arthur, who crushed him in a hug, too. "You look well, Tom. It's good to have my great-great-great-something relatives join me on Vivian's mad quest." He hugged Beansprout too, lifting her off her feet.

"Are you two drunk?" Beansprout asked, suspicious. "You're very merry!"

"Can't I just be pleased to see my friends?" Arthur asked, sitting down at the table and picking up his beer again, and gesturing them to sit, too.

Now that he was reunited with all four of his closest friends in the Otherworld—or anywhere else, really—Tom felt truly at home. Although Tom had grown in the short time they'd been apart, Woodsmoke and Arthur were both still taller than him—Woodsmoke lean and rangy, his longbow propped next to him at the table, and Arthur muscular, Excalibur in its scabbard at his side.

"Let's get more drinks to celebrate," Arthur suggested, and called to the barman. "Five pints of Red Earth Thunder Ale, please!"

As they sat, Beansprout asked, "So, how long have you been here?"

"It took us longer to get here than we thought," Woodsmoke answered. "We wanted to make sure none of the other villages had seen Nimue, so we only arrived here this morning, and decided we needed to recover after our long days on the road." He paused as their ale arrived, and took a long drink as if to emphasise his need to recuperate.

Arthur nodded. "Yes, I wasn't entirely sure Vivian had given us accurate information, but it seems for once, she has. And she's suggested that Nimue stayed at The Hollow Bole—apparently, it's where she's stayed before. That's where I'll be going soon, to ask a few questions." He looked at Tom. "Do you want to come?"

"Yes," Tom said, spluttering his drink in an effort to answer. "But first, tell me what happened with Vivian."

"Ah!" Arthur said, gazing into his pint, "Vivian. It was very strange to meet her again, after so many years. I felt quite sick seeing that big, bronze, dragon-headed prow gliding out of the mist." He sighed, trying to organise his story. "I met her by the lake, at her request. I'd wanted to contact her, but didn't know how. I thought that standing at the lakeside, yelling into the mist probably wouldn't work. But then I had these images enter my dreams, about the standing stones and the lakeside."

"Oh, yes," Tom interrupted. "I've experienced those!"

"So I headed to the lake, and within an hour the boat was there, and then almost instantly she was at my side. She looked so old, and yet so young." He looked up at the others, as if trying to make them see what he had. "I couldn't believe her hair was white! It used to be a rich dark brown that glinted with red when it caught the sunlight. She had freckles then, all over her nose and cheeks." He shook himself out of his reverie as his friends watched him, fascinated by what he must be remembering. "She asked me if I remembered her sisters, the other priestesses, particularly Nimue, which I did. Nimue helped me rule when Merlin disappeared. Vivian explained that she had vanished on her way to Dragon's Hollow to see Raghnall, the dragon enchanter—whoever he is. She was taking her time, visiting various people along the way. The last time Vivian heard from her was when she was here. It's another week's travel to Dragon's Hollow, but she never arrived there."

"And how does Vivian know she hasn't arrived?" Beansprout asked.

"Because Raghnall contacted Vivian, by scrying, to find out where Nimue was. Apparently, Vivian has been trying to contact her ever since, also by scrying, which is apparently how they communicate long distance. Now, Vivian thinks she's being blocked, either by Nimue or someone else."

"What's Nimue like?" Tom asked.

"Oh, she's very different to Vivian. She's small and dark-haired, like a pixie, very pretty. Merlin was infatuated with her," Arthur said thoughtfully. "Vivian is worried that something is wrong, so we've spent the last few days trying to track her route, but we've found nothing of interest. It all seems a wild goose chase," he said, finishing his pint. "So, Tom, shall we go? Woodsmoke looks too comfortable to move." He frowned at Woodsmoke, who had his feet up on a chair looking very relaxed.

"It's been a busy few weeks," Woodsmoke said, indignant. "And I'm much older than you are, so I deserve to relax. Besides, I also have news to catch up on," he added, gesturing to Brenna and Beansprout. He waved them off. "Enjoy your afternoon."

Tom and Arthur set off on a slow, circuitous route.

"I know I've been here a few months now, Tom, but I still can't get used to the place."

Tom nodded. "I know what you mean. Everything is so odd!"

Strange creatures bustled across the square, some tall, others small, male and female, some part human, part animal. They passed a group of satyrs and felt small by comparison. The satyrs were over seven feet tall, with muscular bodies, their upper half bare-chested, the lower half with the hairy legs of goats. Their hair was thick and coarse, large curling rams' horns protruded from their heads, and their eyes were a disconcerting yellow that made them look belligerent. Tom and Arthur skirted past them, making their way to a row of buildings at the side of the square. These were a mixture of shops, semi-permanent markets, eating places, and inns, ranging from the small and shabby to the large and less shabby. Smoke from braziers drifted through the still air.

They looked at the wooden signs that hung from the entrances, trying to find The Hollow Bole.

The pair had been looking for nearly an hour, taking their time drifting through the warren of buildings, before they had any joy. Walking down the start of one of the Holloways, they saw a vast tree to their left, pressing against the bank at its back. There was a narrow cleft in its trunk, above which a small sign announced The Hollow Bole. Peering upwards through the leaves, they saw small windows scattered along thick and misshapen branches. Ducking to avoid hitting their head on the low entrance, they stepped into a small hall hollowed out of the trunk and followed the narrow, spiralling stairs upwards into the gloom. They emerged into a larger hall built into a broad branch overlooking the Holloway and the edge of the square. There were no straight lines anywhere. Instead, the chairs, tables, and balcony were an organic swirl of living wood.

A dryad, green-skinned and willowy, stepped out of the shadows and asked, "Can I help you?"

Thinking they were alone, Tom jumped. Arthur remained a little more composed and said, "I'm looking for an old friend who passed through here, probably a few weeks ago now. Can you confirm if she stayed here?"

"And what do you want with this friend?" the dryad snapped.

"She hasn't arrived where she should have, and I want to find out if anything has happened to her," Arthur replied, trying to keep the impatience out of his voice.

The dryad went silent for a moment. "It depends who it is. Her name?"

"Nimue. Our mutual friend, Vivian, asked me to find her. She's worried."

The dryad was startled. "Nimue? The witch?" She spat out witch viciously.

Now Arthur was startled. "Yes, Nimue, one of the priestesses of Avalon. Or witch, as you choose to call her."

"They are all witches on Avalon," the dryad replied disdainfully. "Yes, she stayed here for a few days. And then she left. I don't know where she went," she added, to avoid further questions.

Arthur groaned. "She gave no indication at all of where she might be going?"

"She stays here because we are discreet. We ask no questions of our clients."

"But you know her well? She stays here often, I believe."

"Not often. She travels less frequently now. But yes, I think she usually stays here. However, I do not know her well. I do not ask questions."

Tom was curious about the word now, and clearly Arthur was, too.

"But she used to travel here more frequently? In the past?" Arthur persisted.

The dryad was visibly annoyed at the constant questions. "Yes, many years ago. But, I do not see what that has to do with now—and I was not here then."

"So if you weren't here then, how do know she came here?" Arthur asked.

"Her name appears in our past registers. We are an old establishment. And her reputation precedes her."

Now Arthur was clearly very curious, and he leaned in. "What reputation?"

"As a witch from another world. A meddler in the affairs of others."

"What affairs?"

"Witches meddle with the natural order of nature!" the dryad snapped, now furious. "As a dryad, I am a natural being, born of the earth and all her darkest mysteries. Witches plunder that knowledge! They have no respect for natural laws. How do you know her?"

Arthur looked uncomfortable, and decided not to answer that. "I am just an old friend who cares for her safety. I am sorry to have taken so much of your time. Are you sure you don't remember anything else?"

"Nothing."

"Just one more question. Did she ever stay here with anyone else?"

"Yes. The greatest meddler of them all—Merlin." With that, she stepped back into the shadows and melted into the tree trunk, becoming invisible and unreachable.

"With Merlin?" Arthur turned to Tom dumbfounded, his face pale at this unexpected news.

Tom felt a thrill run through him at the mention of Merlin, but why was Arthur so upset? Before he could ask, Arthur turned and raced down the stairs. Tom raced after him. Maybe it was because Merlin had travelled here, to the Meet, Tom reflected. It was probably quite unexpected.

Arthur was halfway back to the Quarter Way House before Tom caught up with him. "Arthur, what's the matter?"

"Everything!"

"What do you mean, everything?" Tom asked, even more confused.

Arthur didn't answer, and instead headed to their inn, ran up the stairs, and banged on what Tom presumed was their shared room door.

"Yes? I'm here and I'm not deaf! Come in, the door's open."

But Arthur was already in, throwing the door wide open and striding across the room.

"What's the matter with you?" Woodsmoke asked, alarmed. He was sitting on a chair on the small balcony overlooking the square.

Tom followed Arthur, closing the door behind him, while Arthur sat agitatedly beside Woodsmoke. "Nimue used to come here with Merlin."

Looking confused, Woodsmoke asked, "Is that good or bad?"

"I don't know," Arthur said, confused. "Both? Neither? It's just odd. It's a shock, that's all."

"But this was a long time ago? She wasn't here with him recently?" Woodsmoke asked.

"No, no, of course not. He disappeared years ago. Well, not so long ago for me, merely a few years. But even so, it's a surprise."

"Why? You said they knew each other."

"Yes, but to know that they were here! Together! I didn't think she liked him. She actively avoided him at first, I think." Arthur looked troubled as he tried to recall the nature of their relationship.

"So, you're shocked because you didn't think they knew each other well?" Woodsmoke asked, trying to get to the root of Arthur's problem, and looking further confused in the process.

"Yes," Arthur said. "And now it seems they knew each other better than I realised. Merlin had a sort of obsession with Nimue, but she used to keep him at a distance. Of course, he was much older than her at the time, an old man. A very grumpy, unkempt old man. Still powerful, of course. And she was young and very beautiful. I saw her more often than Vivian—she represented Vivian and Avalon at Camelot. It was there that Merlin first met her." Arthur gazed into the middle distance as he tried to remember the details. "But he could be charming. And he never stopped trying to impress her."

"So, maybe he finally managed to charm her into friendship."

"Maybe. I think she was impressed with his powers, if nothing else. Perhaps that's what swayed her? Maybe they did become good friends?" he mused.

"What powers did Merlin have?" Tom asked. He sat on the floor of the balcony, leaning back against the railing, watching the exchange.

"He was a shape-shifter. He favoured fish and stags, but he could turn into anything he chose. And he had the power of prophecy. But he could perform other magic and spells. I gather he learnt much from travelling here. Obviously, the dryad at The Hollow Bole did not approve of either Merlin or Nimue."

Woodsmoke looked puzzled. "Why not?"

"She said they meddled in the natural order. She seemed to prize her own natural magical abilities far more highly."

"Maybe because their magic is acquired. And of course, they are human."

"Perhaps. Although, I believe Merlin was born with his powers of prophecy and shape-shifting. The rumours were that nobody knew who his father was." Arthur shrugged. "I don't know. Merlin always guarded his secrets closely. He didn't like to share where he was going or what he was doing."

"Perhaps he bewitched Nimue?" Woodsmoke asked.

Arthur looked up sharply. "No, I find that hard to believe. Although," he said thoughtfully, "he was not averse to doing things that would benefit him." He shot off his chair and paced up and down. "You cannot understand how odd this is for me! I have been dead—or asleep, whatever you choose to call it—for hundreds and hundreds of years, but for me that time was only months ago. And yet all of my friends are dead and buried, my kingdom has disappeared, my home is gone, and I am a myth! It's as if I never existed, as Beansprout and Tom told me." He gestured vaguely in Tom's direction. "No evidence that I ever existed at all! As if I am a mere shadow. But then I find that Vivian is still alive, that Morgan was alive, albeit in some other form, and now Nimue! Such unnatural lifespans! And Merlin disappeared hundreds of years ago, but the dryad spoke as if he had just left the room." Deflated, he sat down again. "I don't think I will ever get used to this."

Woodsmoke seemed to take this outburst in his stride, as if he expected it. "I'm sorry, Arthur. I can only imagine how confusing this must be for you. But I thought you liked your chance at another life?"

"I did, and I suppose I still do, most of the time. But today has made me reconsider. However, there isn't much I can do about it. This is my fate, and I must live with it."

Chapter 3 Nimue's Secret

In the end, Tom had left Arthur with Woodsmoke, heading to the bathroom where he had a long cool bath, glad to wash off the dust from the road. Tom couldn't help but feel a little left out. Arthur and Woodsmoke had obviously become good friends in the time they had spent together, and Arthur trusted Woodsmoke's judgement.

They met Brenna and Beansprout back in the bar for their evening meal, Arthur still shaken by the news he had heard. "Did you find out anything on your way here?" he asked Brenna.

"Nothing," she answered. "Many of the people we asked had no idea who Nimue was, and no one had seen a woman travelling alone. Sorry."

"It's all right," Woodsmoke said, distributing the drinks the barman brought over. "We always knew this would be tricky."

"So what now?" Beansprout asked.

Arthur huffed. "Well, seeing as that dryad wouldn't tell me anything, we still have plenty to find out. I can't believe how unhelpful she was!"

"I think she was annoyed by your constant questions, Arthur," said Tom.

"How can I find out anything if I don't ask questions?" said Arthur. "Anyway, we haven't spoken to everyone here yet. Lots of people pass through, so it's worth us staying for another day or two."

"I'll fly over the surrounding area," Brenna said. "See if I can spot anyone who looks like Nimue."

"Thanks, I was hoping you'd offer," Arthur said. "In the meantime, we'll split up and cover the rest of the Meet, and hopefully we'll find out something. Woodsmoke and Beansprout, if you two can cover from the Hollow Bole to the Merry Satyr, Tom and I will do the rest."

"Sure," Woodsmoke said, "whatever you need."

"I'm looking forward to exploring this place," Beansprout said, studying the menu. "And maybe we should try to get some more clothes while we're here, Tom? It would help us both blend in more."

"Good idea, Beansprout," Arthur said. "It will be my treat, Tom. I am no longer a pauper; Vivian is paying me."

"I have a suggestion, Beansprout," Woodsmoke said quietly as Arthur was ordering some food. "Arthur managed to upset the dryad in The Hollow Bole, but I think we should try again. Perhaps a subtler approach by a pleading female friend would have more success."

"Sneaky!" exclaimed Beansprout, "Yes, let's. Nimue must have said something."

The next morning after breakfast they split up. Arthur decided they were going to visit every inn and drinking place – the darker and more secretive-looking, the better.

"Do you think Nimue was up to something?" Tom asked, after they'd just left a particularly seedy bar.

"Not originally, but I think she found out something that has spooked her. She's either gone into hiding, or she's gone to deal with whatever it is." He headed inside another dubious place and Tom realised he'd never get a better education than this. At least his mother would never know.

They had no luck in any of the dark dank inns. They were treated with suspicion and received nothing but grunting shakes of the head. It was only when they stopped at a stall in the village square that they began to get somewhere. Drawn by the smell of meat roasting over a smoky fire, they gazed at the char-grilled chunks of beef and lamb.

"Feeling hungry?" asked the stall owner, a small dwarf-like creature with the ears and muzzle of a dog. He stood on a large box behind his counter, beneath a flapping striped awning.

"Yes, I am!" Arthur declared. "Asking questions is hungry work. Lots of that, that and that," he said, pointing, "for two."

"So what you been asking that's worn you out so much?" said the owner as he sorted out their food.

"My good friend Nimue was meant to meet me here, but I'm very late and she has already gone, without leaving me a note or anything." Arthur shrugged dramatically. "I'm trying to find out where she could have gone so that I can catch up with her." Then for good measure he added, "Women!"

"I know Nimue," the stall owner answered, passing over plates of steaming meats and crusty bread. "She likes my food. She says it's the best in the Meet."

"Does she now!" Arthur said, his mouth full of food.

Tom stood next to him, also cramming in food as if they hadn't had a huge breakfast only a short time before.

"Oh yes, comes here most days when she's in the village. She likes the Bole for a bed, but always grabs snacks from here. Especially for the road. I bag it all up for her, special like, to keep. She'd got a long journey ahead of her last time."

Arthur almost choked in his excitement and Tom intervened, slapping him hard between his shoulder blades.

"It's good to know you're looking out for her," said Arthur. "We worry when she has so far to travel on her own. Did she mention where she was heading? We might still be able to catch up with her."

"Beyond Cervini land, I know that much. You know the Cervini?"

"Not really, we're new here."

"They're shifters. Part deer, part man, sort of. They change between the two."

"Like the Aerikeen?" Tom asked, confused.

"You know them? Yes, just like that! I was here when she met that man."

"What man's that?" Tom asked, trying to be calm.

"Just a traveller passing through. They were both here, getting food and having an idle chat. He was the scruffiest-looking man. Must have been on the road for weeks." He broke off, deep in thought.

Arthur was anxious to keep the story going. "So what were they chatting about?"

"Nimue noticed he had this big dirty dressing on his arm. She asked him about it, and he said he'd been caught in a rock fall up on Scar Face Fell, on the moors beyond White Woods. It's wild land up there, forever in the mists. There'd been a landslip after days of rain – he'd been trying to find shelter in one of the caves, when all of a sudden the rocks fell and he was nearly crushed. Then, lucky for him, this new cave opens up in the hillside behind him."

He paused to serve another customer, and Tom and Arthur bit back their impatience. Once he'd gone, Arthur asked, "So what then?"

"Nimue went dead white when he told his tale. I had to sit her down, looked like she might faint. Strange, she never struck me as the sensitive type before. She asked him if he went in the new cave, and he said yes, but it proved to be many caves and he was afraid of getting lost so he gave up, staying in the main one instead. As soon as the weather got better, he left."

"So is that where she went? Scar Face Fell?"

"I reckon so. She said his story reminded her of something from when she was younger, and it might be nice to go and see the place again. Long way to go if you ask me!"

"Are you sure she didn't mention anything else? Anywhere else?"

"No. Just said she'd need some more supplies, and asked me to prepare some food for her to take. She came to pick it up, and that was the last I saw of her."

Tom and Arthur arrived back at the inn an hour or two later. True to his word, Arthur had helped Tom buy more clothing, and they now carried an assortment of packages. They found Woodsmoke and Beansprout sitting at a quiet corner table in the bar, well away from others, their heads together as they examined a map spread out in front of them. Their hands were cupped around half-empty glasses and the menus were pushed to the side of the table. Arthur and Tom bought drinks and joined them, Tom piling the chair next to him with his packages.

"Looks like you've been successful. Anything in particular you're looking for?" Arthur asked.

"Don't get too excited," Woodsmoke said. "All we know is that Nimue confirmed to the dryad at the Bole that she was changing her plans. She said she'd received news of an old friend and wanted to see if she could find him, and that she wanted to get there before the weather worsened." He gestured at the map. "We were trying to work out where she may have gone."

"An old friend? Interesting, considering what we have heard. And what do you mean, the dryad. She was damn unhelpful to me!"

"As suspected, you obviously didn't know how to ask properly," Beansprout said. "She was extremely lovely to me. And what have you found out?"

"Nimue heard about a rock fall up beyond the White Woods of the Cervini, and it seemed to shock her. Frighten her, even." Arthur related the story they'd heard from the stall owner.

"Why would that frighten her?" Woodsmoke asked.

"We don't know." Tom shrugged. "Maybe she knew something about those caves? She seemed keen to know if the traveller had explored them or found anything there."

"Or anyone there? News of an old friend ..." Arthur looked thoughtful and then worried. "I wonder if this is to do with Merlin."

Woodsmoke looked at Arthur with a suspicious frown. "Merlin! I think you're becoming obsessed with him, Arthur."

"No, no. Hear me out. Merlin disappeared years ago. According to Nimue he walked into the Caledonian woods – in our world, not yours – and never came out. She said at the time that he'd needed some time to himself. But later, now I think about it, her story changed. She said he became threatening – that they'd argued and she had fled. But he

33

never reappeared. Now that in itself is odd; he knew those woods well. He couldn't have got lost, so what happened to him?"

"Didn't you look for him?"

"I couldn't. For a while I didn't even think about it; Merlin was always disappearing for months at a time. Nimue stepped in as my advisor, and I was busy with court affairs, as usual. Not long after, I found out that my best friend had betrayed me, and so I had other things to worry about." He paused and stared at the table, as if to summon his courage. "He'd been having an affair with my wife. When he knew I'd found out, he fled the court, and in a mad rage I raced after him. When I came back, Mordred, my nephew, had seized control of the country and we went to war. And then I died, and you know the rest …"

They fell into an awkward silence, Tom wondering what on earth to say after that. Then, a thought banished everything else from his mind. Slapping the table, he shouted, "I've been so stupid!"

The others jumped, and people sitting close by turned to stare. "Sorry," he said, lowering his voice again, "but I've just remembered. In some of the stories I read about Arthur, it says that Nimue imprisoned Merlin!"

"What? And you've only just remembered?" Beansprout said, looking incredulous.

"There are hundreds, if not thousands, of stories about Arthur and his knights! And some of the names and characters double up just to add to confusion. And I read them years ago!"

Arthur leaned across the table. "What do mean, hundreds of stories about me? You said I was a myth. That no one knew if I ever really existed at all."

34

"That didn't stop the stories, or the fact that you're a national hero."

"I am?" Arthur asked, looking mollified and a little smug.

"Yes," Tom said, grinning. "But to go back to Nimue, there are several versions. Merlin was besotted with her. Completely obsessed. Finally, she had enough of his attentions, but before leaving she decided to learn as much magic as she could from him first. When he was no longer of use, she either imprisoned him in a tomb in the middle of the forest, or in a cave, or in a crystal tower that she made, which then became invisible. Most stories say he was imprisoned alive, but then died. But obviously, who would ever know? None of the stories suggest he reappeared after you died, Arthur. I think." He shrugged. "When you died, that was the end of everyone's story."

The others looked dumbfounded. Woodsmoke stirred first. "So this could be about Merlin. What better way to ensure he was never found than by imprisoning him here?"

"… in the Scar Face Fell caves," Beansprout said. "And now they are exposed, she's worried he'll be found!"

"But surely he'd be dead?" Tom said.

"Nimue is not convinced, obviously. She's gone to find him."

Their discussion was interrupted by the arrival of Brenna, and she slid into a chair next to them. "Oh good, I've found you. I thought you'd be here," she said, smiling wryly.

"How did you get on?" Arthur asked.

"Badly. No sign of Nimue. There were no women travelling alone. But I flew close to every group I passed, to check who was travelling with them. No one matched Nimue's description. What about you?"

35

"We found out a lot," Arthur answered. "I'm sorry you had a useless trip, though."

"No, it's fine. It was good to be able to fly." She starting laughing, "You look like you're going to burst, Arthur! What have you found out?"

"She's gone to find Merlin! In Scar Face Fells."

Brenna looked at the others, then back at Arthur. "Merlin. Your Merlin?"

"Yes. She's been the one responsible for his disappearance all along." Arthur was flushed and excited, glad to share his news.

"We think," cautioned Woodsmoke.

"Did you like Nimue, Arthur?" Brenna asked.

He looked surprised by the question. "Yes, of course. I had no reason to suspect her of anything until now. She was always very helpful."

She seemed reassured. "Good. I'm glad we've made progress." She pulled the map towards her and ran her finger across the map. "Scar Face Fell. That's quite a way. I presume that's where we're going next, then?

"Absolutely; we have to follow her," Arthur said, a determined look settling across his face. "But we'll need supplies."

Woodsmoke nodded. "Let's make a list. We can get everything this afternoon, and leave first thing tomorrow."

"You're with me then?" Arthur asked, looking at them one by one.

"Of course," Tom answered, barely able to contain his excitement. "We're talking about finding Merlin and Nimue!"

"Good," Arthur said, clearly pleased. "Let's order some food and plan our route. If there's a chance he's alive, I have to save him."

Chapter 4 The Chase

They left the Meet on the north-west Holloway that led out of the meadowlands and into the hills. This path continued on to the White Woods of the Cervini and then the fells. Woodsmoke had warned them the land would get rougher and the weather colder as they travelled higher. They had bought thick travelling cloaks and extra blankets, and for shelter, a large circular sheet of sewn-together tanned hides, and a thick wooden pole.

"Is that a tent?" Tom had asked when they bought it.

"Of a fashion," Woodsmoke said. "At least it will provide us with some protection when the weather worsens."

"I thought you always had good weather here. Isn't it called the summer country?"

"It is by some. But places still vary, and the higher we go, the colder it gets."

Woodsmoke had strapped the pole awkwardly behind him on his horse, along with the bulky mass of the tent. They were all similarly heavily laden, their saddlebags bulging with supplies of dried meats, cheese, fruits, and extra clothing.

None of them were familiar with the places they were travelling to, but for Tom and Beansprout this was an exciting chance to learn more of the Other. They had pored over the map, reading the strange names as they traced their route.

"Who are the Cervini?" Beansprout asked as they trekked along.

"They are shapeshifters, like me," Brenna said, "but they turn into deer rather than birds. They live in the White Woods."

"Merlin was fond of turning into a stag," Arthur said. "It was his favourite animal form. That might explain why he would travel here with Nimue – they would have seemed like family."

"So some of them may know him?" Tom asked.

Woodsmoke grimaced. "I suppose so. But it was a long time ago since anyone last saw Merlin."

"I wonder how they would feel if they knew he might still be alive?" Tom said thoughtfully. "And I wonder if some of them would know Nimue?" he added as an afterthought.

Tom woke up with a crick in his neck. Light was beginning to seep through the thick tanned hide, illuminating the flap that served as the tent entrance. He sat up slowly and quietly, unwilling to wake the others. He glanced round at the various-sized humps covered in blankets that snuffled and snored gently, cramped in the confined space, and wrinkled his nose at the musty smell that filled the air. Easing his legs from beneath his blankets, he made his way out of the tent.

The sky was low and heavy with thick grey clouds, and a brisk wind blew across the hills. Their surroundings were springing into shape as the light increased, revealing the flat sheltered area in the curve of a hillside where they had set up camp. The grass was shaggy and tufted, broken by small stones, and had been uncomfortable to sleep on. The meadowlands and Holloways were a lush green in the distance.

They had been travelling for over a week, making good time, and were now not far from the Cervini lands. Yesterday, after they had set up camp, Brenna had flown over the White Woods, and on towards Scar Face Fell. She returned with interesting news. Although she hadn't seen Nimue, a herd of stags had gathered at a point midway along the long stretch of pitted and pock-marked rock that rose out of the moor, exposed by centuries of wind and rain. Some of the cliff faces were tall and imposing, towering menacingly over the landscape, while others were low, barely twice the height of a man. They ran in a continuous ragged chain, scarring the lowlands for miles.

"I hadn't realised how big they are," she said on her return. "We would have been searching for weeks!"

"You think the stags have found something? Merlin?" Arthur asked eagerly.

"They've found something. Some were in human form; they were heading in and out of a cave entrance. And there did look to have been a rock fall. I have no idea how recently, though."

"It must be Merlin. What else could they have found?"

Woodsmoke had been stirring the stew which was bubbling over the fire, but he looked up. "Who knows what they do there, Arthur. It could be where they bury their dead."

"No, I don't believe in coincidences." Arthur pulled the map out of his pack. "Are the Cervini aggressive?"

"Not that I'm aware. Not needlessly, anyway," Woodsmoke answered.

Arthur ran his finger over the map, tracing routes and muttering to himself. After a few minutes he looked up. "I think we should split up, but I'm going to think on it, and we'll discuss it in the morning."

Woodsmoke had looked as if he were going to say more, but instead he returned to the food, an uneasy look on his face.

Not long after that they had rolled into bed, and now, as Tom prodded the smouldering fire in the dawn stillness, he wondered what their strategy would be. He pulled his heavy cloak round his shoulders and smiled as he thought over the past few days. Arthur had assumed a fatherly role that Tom found disconcerting, but also reassuring. He had continued teaching him how to sword fight, lessons that had begun weeks before, but had been interrupted by his to trip to see Brenna. He maintained it was a skill Tom should learn. He'd bought Tom a sword from one of the stalls in the Meet – slightly smaller and lighter than Excalibur, and easier for him to handle – and they practised every evening.

After a clumsy start, some of the skills he'd learnt started to return, but it was going to take time. "It's all right, Tom," Arthur had reassured him, "I started to learn as a child, but you'll get there."

Brenna and Woodsmoke would join in, but Beansprout practised using the longbow she usually wore slung behind her back. Woodsmoke had taught her to use it, and every now and again he would break off and watch her progress, adjusting her stance and her grip. It had taken Tom a while to get used to seeing her with a bow; it only reinforced how different things here were from at home.

A rustling sound disturbed his thoughts, and Arthur wriggled free of the tent to sit next to him. "Morning, Tom, you're up early," he said softly to avoid waking the others.

"I didn't sleep well, stiff neck," Tom said, rolling his shoulders.

Arthur laughed. "Ah, life on the road."

"Have you decided what we're going to do?"

"I've decided that we – me and you – should cross the Cervini land and head towards the fells. It's more direct and will get us there quicker, but we may be stopped and questioned. The others should go the longer way round and hang back to see what's happening. That way, if we get caught, we've got back up. Brenna can keep an eye on things."

"When you say 'caught', do you mean imprisoned?" Tom asked, alarmed.

"I hope not, but you never know."

"But why would they imprison us, if we're only passing through? Woodsmoke said it would be fine."

"It depends what they're up to. I'd actually like to run into them so we can ask them about Nimue." He thought for a moment, then said, "Unless of course we travel to the White Woods and seek them out, to ask if they've seen her passing through."

Tom watched as Arthur gazed into space, a furrow between his brows as he worked through his options. "No, it will take too long, and we know where she's going. Let's press on." He smiled at Tom. "We're getting close."

When the others woke up and joined them around the fire, it was apparent they weren't impressed with the idea of splitting up, and there was a general chorus of disapproval, but Arthur shrugged their protests off.

Woodsmoke however wasn't prepared to drop it. As they packed up he said, "There's strength in numbers, we should stay together. Or at least we should cross Cervini lands and you should go the long way round."

"No. I'd rather take the risks than you," Arthur told him. Tom could tell he was excited at the thought of action, and had no intention of being relegated to a safe role. "Besides, there's really no risk. You said they weren't dangerous."

"But I don't know that for sure!" Woodsmoke glared at Arthur. "Besides, it's not just you who's at risk."

Arthur turned to Tom expectantly. "You'll be fine, won't you Tom?"

"Of course," Tom said, not willing to upset either Arthur or Woodsmoke.

Brenna interrupted. "I suppose the suggestion does make some sense, Woodsmoke. If for some reason one group is delayed, the other can continue the search."

"That's settled then," Arthur said, not giving Woodsmoke time to respond. "I'm sure we'll meet up at the cave with no problems. And Brenna can keep on eye things, right Brenna?"

"Of course. But be careful, Arthur!"

Woodsmoke stood by his horse, adjusting his packs and brooding silently. When he couldn't contain himself any longer, he rounded on Arthur. "This is rash! We don't know where Nimue is. She could already be there. She could put a spell on you two, or all of us, and then what?"

"And this is why we're splitting up! Besides, she won't put a spell on us," Arthur said, rolling his eyes.

"She's hiding her actions from everyone, Arthur. She's obviously panicking; she's abandoned all her plans! She's even avoiding Vivian! We have no idea what she's capable of.

Or what she's done. Everything we think we know is pure guesswork."

"It's good guesswork and you know it."

Arthur and Woodsmoke stopped packing and stared at each other across the smoking remains of the fire.

"My point is, Arthur," Woodsmoke said, slowly and deliberately, "you seem to be in a rush to get to Merlin without considering anything else. If the Cervini have found Merlin, what are they doing there? What do they want with him? What if they are working with Nimue? We'll be outnumbered. We need to find out more before we go stumbling into this! Remember, we were only supposed to be finding Nimue."

Arthur answered, as slowly as Woodsmoke, "This is now about much more than just Nimue."

"For you."

"If Vivian knew–"

"She doesn't," Woodsmoke interrupted. "And you don't know what she'd think."

"I know her better than you do. This is not a discussion. We'll split up and meet at the rock face by the entrance to the cave. Or as close to it as we can get, depending on the Cervini. Brenna can liaise between us."

There was silence as Woodsmoke stared at Arthur. "I think the prospect of you possibly finding Merlin is skewing your judgement. When we get to the rock face, you'd better wait for us before doing anything." Woodsmoke strode to his horse and finished packing in silence.

For the next few hours of riding, no one spoke. Woodsmoke rode ahead, and when they eventually split up, his final words were, "Remember to wait, Arthur."

Chapter 5 Scar Face Fell

Tom and Arthur travelled for the rest of the day without seeing anyone. The land rose higher and the heavy grey skies seemed to get lower and lower, until they felt squashed between them. A stiff breeze flattened the grass, and the chill made Tom pull his cloak closer around him.

In the distance, the White Woods appeared as a white haze of trees brooding over the windswept landscape. Arthur stopped for a minute to watch the tree line, but nothing moved and no one emerged, so they pressed on, Tom trying to ignore the woods and whatever they might contain.

At dusk they saw the craggy edge of the fells, breaking up the horizon into a jagged unwelcoming mass. Arthur pushed on despite the failing light, keen to find shelter from the unrelenting wind, as the others had the tent. The horses slowed to a weary trot, picking their way carefully over the broken ground, and eventually, as night fell, they stumbled into a rocky enclave marking the start of the fells.

The wind dropped immediately, replaced by an eerie silence. It was as if they had fallen into a dark pit. Tom could just make out Arthur's figure as he slid from his horse to the ground, calling, "Wait there, Tom."

Tom heard him scrabbling in his panniers, and then torchlight flared and the darkness scattered to reveal a small irregularly shaped space enclosed by rock and open to the night sky. The floor was covered with dry flattened grass. There were three other exits, opposite to where they had entered.

Tom dismounted and lit his own torch, waiting as Arthur investigated the other exits. It was unnerving being on his own, and in the silence Tom became jumpy. He rummaged for some dried meats to chew on and patted Midnight, not sure who was more reassured by this comforting gesture.

After an interval of several interminable minutes, Arthur reappeared. "Two of them are just small passageways snaking through the rocks, but through this one," he gestured behind him, "there's a sheltered rocky hollow where we can light a fire."

"What's wrong with staying here?" Tom asked, thinking it was a good place to settle for the night.

"It's too close to the entrance. Follow me."

They led their horses down the passage, the harsh clop of hooves echoing off the stone, and after a few minutes came to a circular space protected on all sides by a rock wall. They secured the horses, then lit a fire beneath an overhanging rock. Arthur opened a bottle of dark ale from the inn, and after taking a drink passed it to Tom. He took a deep draught, feeling it warming and relaxing him.

Tom was shattered, aching from the long days of riding, the constant wind and uncomfortable sleeping. He rummaged in his pack and took out more dried meats, cheeses and bread, then settled his pack behind him and tried to get comfortable. Arthur sat staring into the fire, deep in thought. Tom nudged him, holding out some food. "Here, Arthur, you should eat."

He looked round startled. "Sorry, Tom. Miles away. I don't know about you, but I think we just rest tonight, no training."

"That's fine by me," Tom said, relieved. "What do you think will happen? Will we find Merlin?"

Arthur shook his head. "I don't know. Now we're so close, it feels unreal, especially considering how long it's been. The reality of us actually finding him seems unlikely."

"But the Cervini have found something."

"That could be anything. It's just wishful thinking on my behalf. Just like one of those old tales you've been reading."

"But those tales turned out to be true, didn't they?" Tom smiled. "I'm sitting with a living legend. I'm actually related to you!" he said smugly.

Arthur laughed. "Yes, you are. And it's Merlin's doing that you're here now."

"Just think," Tom mused, "if I ever went back to my Earth, I could write the real story of Arthur. And your new tales!"

"But you're not going back," Arthur said, frowning.

"No, I'm not. It's just a thought." Tom took another swig of beer and wriggled into his cloak. "Do you miss your Earth?"

"Yes and no. I miss my friends, my home, but I don't miss war or bloodshed. Or endless decisions of policy and state. It's curious, though, not to have everyone hanging on your every word, looking to you to make every decision."

Tom wondered if he'd mention Woodsmoke and their argument earlier, but Arthur just sighed deeply. "It's actually quite liberating. I have a remarkable amount of freedom here, and anonymity. I like that."

"You're not bored, then?"

"Not yet." He said it evenly, but even so, Tom wondered how true that was. Surely it must be hard, going from being a King of Britain to a King of nothing.

During the night, despite his layers of clothing, cloak and blanket, the cold seeped into Tom's bones and he woke chilled. Mist had settled into the hollow, blurring the grey rock walls, and he could feel a faint slick of moisture on his face and hair. He sat up and prodded life back into the fire, then put some water on to boil for herb tea. Looking up, all he could see was white mist. A faint murmur of wind penetrated the unearthly silence. It was if they had passed out of this world and into another.

He felt groggy, as if he'd slept too long. He went to check the time, before remembering he'd taken off his watch and put it in his pack. It didn't work here.

Arthur still lay wrapped in his blankets, looking so comfortable that Tom hesitated to wake him. But he was sure they'd slept later than normal, and that they needed to get moving. He shook him until he roused. "Arthur, wake up."

Tom stood up and stamped his feet to get warm, then wandered over to where the horses were feeding. At least they looked rested. Tom had a nagging doubt about today, and wished they were with the others ... which then made him feel guilty about doubting Arthur.

After a quick breakfast and a hot drink, they set off. The mist remained thick and heavy, and a fine drizzle started to fall, further obstructing their view and muffling all sound. They kept the fells close to their right, the height of the massive stretch of rock lost in the mists. Huge chunks of stone, some the size of buildings, littered the floor, and they wound their way around them, listening carefully for any sign of the Cervini.

They had definitely overslept, and the thick mist delayed them further, so the day was growing steadily darker by the time they heard a low muffled shout. Arthur gestured to Tom to stop, whispering, "Did you hear that?"

Tom nodded. "Yes, but not what was said."

"Let's leave the horses here and proceed on foot." Arthur slipped to the ground and led them behind a large outcrop of fallen rock. They secured the horses and, staying close to the shelter of the rocks, edged their way forward.

They heard another voice, deep and gruff – much closer this time, and edged with amusement. "I think the witch actually looked scared."

"She should be," the first voice called from a short distance away. "Orlas is furious. She'll be lucky to keep her life."

"Well she'd better do what she's told, then," the second voice answered.

Arthur grabbed Tom's arm and pulled him back a few paces, whispering, "We'll be lucky if there's only two on guard. Stay here while I look."

Arthur disappeared into the mist, leaving Tom nervously peering around him at the fallen mounds of rock. The voices sounded like they were coming from just ahead and to the left, but the thick mist distorted everything, and he half-expected a Cervini to walk around the rocks and find him hiding.

Minutes later, Arthur reappeared.

"They're sitting a short distance away, at the top of the rise, with their backs to the cave entrance. There may well be more of them out on the slopes, but I can't see a damn thing in this mist." He grinned unpleasantly. "They obviously don't expect visitors from this direction, so we'll slip quietly behind them and into the caves. Ready?"

"No, not really," Tom said, surprised. "We're supposed to meet the others," he reminded Arthur. "Shouldn't we wait? Brenna will be looking for us."

"She'll never find us in this mist."

"But we promised Woodsmoke. And they could be very close. Especially as we overslept."

Arthur took a deep breath. "Plans change, Tom. We need to act before it's too late. And besides, if this mist has delayed us, it will definitely have delayed them. They could still be hours away."

"But Brenna definitely won't find us if we're in a cave."

"She'll see the horses and work it out. Then she can tell the others."

Tom's earlier uneasiness returned. "But Arthur, we don't know what to expect."

"Yes we do! The witch they referred to is Nimue. She's in there right now, with the Cervini, and not willingly by the sound of it. We cannot afford to wait if we're going to find Merlin."

"But then what? We haven't properly discussed this!"

"We are improvising."

Tom's uneasiness started to turn into panic. Arthur had no intention of waiting for the others, and Tom wondered if he was trying to prove a point to Woodsmoke. He stood implacable, clothed in a slight swagger, one hand on Excalibur, his other reaching to grasp Tom's forearm.

"Come on, Tom, no time for doubts. We'll be fine."

Tom nodded nervously, sensing that Arthur would go anyway, and he knew he'd rather go with Arthur than be alone. "All right," he answered eventually.

"Good, stay close."

Arthur led the way, weaving around the stones, making his way to the rock face. The grass was thick and damp, masking their footfalls, but they kept a hand to their swords just in case. As they rounded a large fallen rock, Tom saw the guards. Their backs were to them and they stood close together, laughing and talking, oblivious to their presence. Arthur gestured to his right, and Tom saw the cave entrance, high and narrow, with darkness beyond.

Chapter 6 Blind Moor

Woodsmoke, Beansprout and Brenna stood tucked beneath the overhang of a large rock, Woodsmoke looking angry and worried.

Poor visibility had threatened to slow their progress, but they had raced recklessly over the uneven ground, Woodsmoke keen to maintain pace despite the mist and drizzle. Brenna had frequently corrected their progress as she flew to and fro, trying to orientate herself.

"I'm sorry, Woodsmoke," Brenna said, "but I cannot see through thick mist. I've flown very low and I still can't see them. But you'll be pleased to know we're close to the cave."

"I knew this would happen!" Woodsmoke said accusingly. "Splitting up was a stupid idea. And you encouraged it."

"I'm sorry, but it did seem a good idea. We had no idea this mist would come down so thickly for so long."

He glared at her and took a deep breath. "Where did you last see them?"

"At the edge of the rocks last night, a few hours' ride from the cave. But it was late and they looked fine, so I left them. I can't see them anywhere today. They should have arrived here hours ago."

"They must be somewhere."

"Of course they're somewhere," she spat.

"Have you seen the Cervini?"

"I can see two at the entrance to the cave, but most of them seem to have gone. The mist–"

"Yes, yes, yes. The mist," he echoed sarcastically. "So you don't know where the Cervini are, or where Tom and Arthur are?"

"No."

"I will go. Wait here." He tossed her his horse's reins and strode off without a backward glance.

Beansprout was concerned. "He's very cross! I've never seen him like this before."

"I have," Brenna said with a sigh. "He's like this when he's worried, and right now he's worried about Tom. And even though he's angry with Arthur, he's worried about him too. However, I would prefer he did not take it out on me."

They fell silent, the mist muffling sight and sound. Beansprout scanned what little she could see of the scrubby grass, heathers and curling ferns crowding together in a thick and luxuriant mass. The two of them waited an uncomfortably long time until Woodsmoke returned.

"They're already in the cave," he said, as he snatched his horse's reins back from Brenna. He was even more furious than before.

Beansprout had a jolt of worry race through her. "What? How do you know?"

"I found their horses tied up a short distance past the cave. And I could smell Tom and Arthur at the cave entrance."

"I can't believe they've gone in alone!" Beansprout saw her own shock echoed on Brenna's face.

"I can. Arthur's doing, of course," Woodsmoke said. "And there's a smell of decay coming from those caves too, of something long buried and forgotten. There are torches inside the entrance, marking the route."

"Are there many Cervini?" Brenna asked.

"The two you saw at the entrance, and another dozen grazing on the moor. I made sure to pass upwind of them, so they couldn't smell me. We did well to circle so far around them," he added in consolation.

Beansprout pulled her cloak tightly around her shoulders as if to fend off bad news, and asked the question she already knew the answer to. "What do we do now?"

"We try to find them," Woodsmoke said grimly.

Chapter 7 Nimue

Tom and Arthur followed the passageway upwards and inwards. The floor was uneven, and only a small amount of light was provided by the intermittent torches, so they stumbled along in near darkness, seeing only a faint orange glow up ahead.

Tom followed close on Arthur's heels, until eventually Arthur came to a sudden stop, and Tom thudded into him. Arthur gestured for silence, and Tom peered round him to see a large cave just ahead. A cluster of torches smoked and flickered in the centre, illuminating a small group of people. They were all male, except for a small woman Tom presumed was Nimue. Arthur and Tom stepped as close to the cave entrance as they dared, careful to remain in the shadows.

Nimue's voice rang out loudly. "How do I know I can trust you? If I release him, what will you do to me?"

"If you don't release him we shall leave you powerless, trapped within the binding spell. And then we will seal you in here. Forever." The man who spoke leaned over her aggressively.

"You should mind your threats, Orlas. In order for me to release Merlin, you must release me from the binding spell. I will have my powers restored."

"Temporarily. Until you prove yourself safe."

"You will have to do better than that. If I release him, you will allow me to leave, no repercussions, and no binding spell. You will have Merlin, and that is what you want, isn't it?"

"Will he be alive?"

She paused as she thought. "I don't know. I sealed him in here out of place and time. He should be alive, but I can't say for sure."

"Where is he?" Orlas turned slowly, looking at the walls and up into the impenetrable blackness of the roof.

Nimue smiled. "You'll see. You'd better release me, Nerian," she said to a tall lean man with a beard and long matted hair.

He turned to Orlas, who shook his head. "Not yet. You will get everything ready first."

Orlas then spoke to the other Cervini: "Set out the torches, and move back to the entrance."

Tom whispered to Arthur, "Should we leave?"

"Not a chance."

"But we'll be caught!"

Tom looked at the cave, wondering where in such a bare place they might be able to hide. As well as Orlas and Nerian, there were another three Cervini, who were now placing five torches in a rough circle around Nimue, who was rummaging in a bag.

Tom and Arthur were so transfixed by the activities in the cave that they failed to hear another Cervini creep up behind them. They were alerted by the hiss of a sword as he pulled it free from his scabbard to hover under Arthur's chin, the point nudging his neck.

Arthur's hand shot to Excalibur, but the Cervini's sword pushed more firmly into his neck and he dropped his hands.

The gruff voice sounded unexpectedly loud. "I think not. One more twitch and I shall remove your head from your shoulders. Orlas!" he shouted. "You should pay better attention to your surroundings. You have visitors."

The others turned to watch as the Cervini, an older man of medium height with short grey hair, pushed Tom and Arthur into the cave, keeping his sword firmly pushed into Arthur's back. Tom edged his hand towards his own sword, but the Cervini just looked at him and tutted. "Now is not the time for heroics," he said softly.

At a nod from Orlas, two more Cervini withdrew their swords and flanked Tom and Arthur.

Orlas stood in front of them, a tall, imposing figure with broad shoulders and powerful arms. Dark hair fell to his shoulders, and in the torchlight they saw strange markings across his skin, and on the skin of the other Cervini – mottled browns, cream and tan, like camouflage. In fact, Tom thought, just like deer.

Orlas looked at Arthur. "Do I know you?"

"No," Arthur answered, "but I know Nimue."

She stepped closer to look at him. Orlas put a restraining hand on her arm, and she shook it off impatiently.

Tom watched, fascinated, as he saw her properly for the first time. She was so small and slender; she barely came up to his shoulders. Her dark hair tumbled across her shoulders and her skin was pale and creamy, but it was her eyes that held him. They were dark green, and utterly captivating.

But she wasn't looking at Tom; in fact, she barely glanced at him.

"Arthur," she said. "After all these years! How did you find me?"

"Vivian sent me. And as you should remember, Nimue, I am very persistent." His voice hardened as he added, "Especially when it comes to Merlin."

"Yes, I remember. Who'd have thought the old man would be so missed?"

Orlas interrupted. "Arthur? Merlin's Arthur? You look remarkably well preserved for a dead man."

"Don't I just?" Arthur answered dryly. "Preservation in a tomb of ice has beneficial consequences. Merlin's last gift."

Orlas nodded at Tom. "Who's this?"

"My rescuer, and also my descendant, Tom."

"I see." Orlas briefly appraised him, leaving Tom feeling uncomfortable, before turning back to Arthur. "And you are here because?"

"Because Nimue disappeared and Vivian – our mutual friend – became worried about her safety. She asked me to find her. Eventually I suspected that Nimue had imprisoned Merlin and was making her way here to ensure he remained in the spell. However, Merlin was like a father to me, and I came here to rescue him and stop Nimue."

"An ally?" Orlas persisted. "You are not here to rescue the witch, then?"

"Definitely not," Arthur said, glaring at Nimue.

"And you're alone?" He looked beyond them to the entrance, as if others would suddenly emerge from the shadows.

"Absolutely," Arthur lied smoothly. Although in reality, Tom thought, he was telling the truth – they had no idea where Woodsmoke and the others were. "We have been tracking Nimue from Holloways Meet."

Orlas looked to the Cervini who had caught them. "Rek?"

"I've seen no one else," he confirmed.

Orlas nodded briefly at the others and they re-sheathed their swords. Tom relaxed; he hadn't realised he'd been standing so stiffly.

"May I ask how you come to be here with Nimue?" Arthur said.

"I found her," Rek answered. "She was cutting across our land, heading towards Scar Face Fell. Ever since Merlin disappeared, we have wondered what happened to him. Nimue was the last person we saw him with, so our laws say that if we ever saw Nimue again, she was to be escorted to the Great Hall for questioning. Fortunately, I have a good memory and I recognised her immediately." He must have seen Tom's startled expression. "I was a very young fawn in those days," he explained.

"You confessed?" Arthur asked, looking at Nimue.

She remained stubbornly silent, leaving Orlas to explain. "No, she did not. In fact she tried to put a spell on those escorting her, but one of them spotted what she was up to and stopped her. Nerian, our shaman, has restricted her powers by using a binding spell. And due to her lack of co-operation …" he smiled and gave a short bow to Nimue, "we have kept her locked in a cell as our guest for a week or so. Eventually our investigations led us here."

Arthur looked around the bare cave. "Are you sure this is the place? It could be a trick."

"It's no trick," Nerian said. "I used a spell tracer and it led us here. Merlin and Nimue entered, but only Nimue left."

"Well, this is all very entertaining," Nimue said, "but are we going to get on with it?" A small smiled played across her lips and Tom couldn't help but feel she had something planned.

"Yes we are. I have no idea how long you have been watching, Arthur, but Nimue is about to lift the spell." Orlas turned back to her. "Continue, Nimue, we are all waiting."

Nimue moved back into the circle of torchlight and took a bundle of herbs from her bag. "This is all I need. You may wish to move back before I begin."

"No." Orlas shook his head. "Nerian and I will wait here. Everyone else should wait in the entrance. Arthur?"

"We remain here too."

Tom stood nervously beside Arthur, wondering what to expect, and not for the first time wished Arthur was a little less headstrong.

"All right then," Orlas said to the shaman. "Remove the binding spell."

Nerian's long matted hair seemed to writhe in the flickering torchlight as he pulled one of many necklaces free from his leather shirt. At the end was tied a small bound doll. Tom suppressed a gasp – it was an uncanny likeness of Nimue. Twisting the doll carefully in his hands, he unwound its leather binding, chanting slowly. He placed the leather strip carefully in his pocket, then snapped his fingers over the doll. A bright blue flame flashed along it and then disappeared.

Nimue took a long deep breath in and out, as if waking from a deep sleep. A ripple passed through her and she seemed to become more alert, more alive.

Orlas nodded at Nerian. "You too, back to the entrance. In case anything goes wrong."

"Wait. The doll." Nimue held out her hand expectantly. At Nerian's hesitation, she said, "Now."

Nerian reluctantly handed it over and retreated to the entrance.

Pocketing the doll, she turned away and started to separate the bundle of herbs. She stepped to the furthest of the torches and, muttering too quietly for anyone to hear, threw some of the herbs into the wavering flame. They burned instantly, and as she continued to mutter her incantations, the flame changed colour from a warm orange to a deep blood red. She thrust the rest of the bundle of herbs into the flames until it caught, and then withdrew it again. The herb bundle burnt steadily without being consumed, and she stepped beyond the circle of torchlight, carrying it around the outskirts of the cave, starting to the left of the entrance.

Tom stood watching her, holding his breath, wondering what would happen. Her movements were sure and steady, and she paced around the room until she had completed a full circle, coming to a stop at the entrance to the cave where she placed the still-burning bundle of herbs on the floor.

Those standing in the entrance looked uncertain. No one said a word. Glancing at Arthur, Tom saw that his eyes were bright with anticipation, but Tom started to have a very bad feeling; it seemed to him that Nimue was blocking the entrance. Was she lifting the spell, or casting another?

She moved past them back into the circle of torchlight, and clapped her hands in a rapid staccato. The cave was suddenly plunged into almost complete darkness, as the torches burnt a deep blood red, painting everything with the colour of death. Then, as if a veil had been lifted from their eyes, the cave transformed into something else entirely.

Chapter 8 The Silver Tower

The cave had vanished. They were standing in ancient woodland, the ground thick with moss. Ahead, on a rocky mound, stood a silver tower that shone in the sunlight, its door and windows flung open. The whole place had an air of desolation and decay.

Tom's skin prickled with unease, which soon turned to alarm as he realised he was standing next to a huge brown bear and a magnificent stag. The bear roared, and Tom backed off quickly, tripping and landing on the ground. But the bear ignored him and padded into the undergrowth. The stag gazed at Tom with liquid brown eyes and then moved off to graze in a patch of sunlight filtering down through the canopy. Tom realised the stag was Orlas, so the bear must be Arthur.

They were enchanted; he was alone.

Tom spun around, trying to orientate himself, but found it was impossible. He felt as if he'd been transported back hundreds of years; something in the air felt old and mysterious. And where were they? Had she transported them out of the cave, or were they still in it? And if he wasn't enchanted, how could he see the grove?

Panicking, Tom looked round for Nimue, and saw her entering the silver tower. He raced to catch up with her, clambering over the rocks to the entrance. Nimue didn't turn round. Ever since the binding spell had been lifted, she'd completely ignored them, as if they were irrelevant.

Tom paused on the threshold, looking up at the tower. He stroked the burnished wall; it really did look like silver. Close up, he could see curious engravings all around the doorway. The door itself was also silver, thick and solid, and beyond it was a sitting room in which a large chair sat next to a fireplace. Despite the sunshine outside, a small fire burned in the grate. Rugs were scattered across the floor, and the room was filled with sunlight reflecting off the silver walls. As the light danced around the room, he was reminded of being underwater in the Emperor's palace when he had visited the Eye.

Opposite him was a staircase, and before he had a chance to change his mind he crossed the room and started climbing the steps.

On the next level was a bedroom, luxuriously furnished with tapestries and rugs, and a bed piled high with pillows. This room was also empty, so he continued up the stairs. At the top was a small landing with a door that was partly closed. He could hear movement behind it, so he eased it open a little further, peering into the room beyond.

It was a workshop, filled with wooden benches, its walls crowded with shelves, and everything stacked high with books and papers, and hundreds of pots and jars of all sizes. Again a fire burned in the fireplace, and a large cauldron was suspended over it.

But this room wasn't empty. On the floor in front of the fire was the inert body of a man. He had long white hair and a thick white beard, and was wearing a long, grey, hooded robe. Crouched by his side was Nimue. Her back was to Tom, but he could see her hand stroking his face. Then her shoulders dropped and she sat back on the floor, her hands cradled in her lap.

Tom wondered what to do. He didn't want to disturb her, but equally he had to know what was happening. And Merlin – because that must be him lying on the floor – appeared to be dead.

He pushed the door open and stepped into the room. Immediately, Nimue leapt to her feet and turned, her hands raised.

"No!" Tom shouted, stepping back a pace. "I just want to talk to you."

She laughed and looked relieved. "Oh, it's you." Then her expression turned confused as she asked, "Why aren't you enchanted, like the others?"

He shrugged. "I have no idea."

"Curious," she said, suddenly interested in him. "You look normal enough. Ah!" she exclaimed. "You must possess a talisman."

Tom wondered what she was talking about. "I don't care. Why have you enchanted the others? Why is Arthur a bear?"

"A bear?" she said, laughing. "That's unexpected. That was his old name, Arturus, because of his bear-like qualities. In magic, we call it his animal spirit. This place, the spell, must have released it. Anyway, they are enchanted because I don't like being threatened."

"Maybe you shouldn't have imprisoned Merlin," Tom answered swiftly. "You've killed him, haven't you?"

She narrowed her eyes at him. "Watch your tongue, boy, or it will soon be mine, talisman or not."

"Is he dead?" he persisted.

"No. That is why the spell still exists. He is unconscious. Unrousable."

Despite the fact he'd never known Merlin, Tom was relieved to know he was still alive. "Where are we?" he asked, slightly mollified.

"Still in the cave, of course," she said, smirking.

"But how can that be? Where is all this coming from?" He gestured around him.

"My magic. Or should I say, Merlin's magic. I asked him to teach me the spell for how to imprison a man, and this is it." She leaned back against the bench, watching him.

"But why is it so ... non-prison-like?" he asked, for want of a better word.

"Foolish boy. People are willing to imprison themselves in all sorts of things as long as it's comfortable enough."

"So, how long has he been lying there?"

"I have no idea. I used to visit him at first, but then I just got bored, and he never seemed to miss me, so ..." Her voice trailed off.

Overcome with curiosity, Tom asked, "Can I see him?"

She shrugged. "If you wish," and she moved aside to let him pass.

He crossed the room and knelt next to Merlin, turning him over to see him properly. He looked as if he was sleeping; an old man who'd dozed off in front of the fire, creases lining his face, his mouth carrying the remnants of a smile. He certainly didn't look like a powerful wizard – not that he knew what one should look like. He felt inexplicably sad, and found himself worried about Arthur, who would be so upset.

Nimue interrupted his thoughts. "There's nothing else I can do, so I'm leaving."

He stood and faced her. "You can't leave us here; we've done nothing to you!" And then he realised that if he was to figure a way out of here, he needed to understand what had happened. "Why are we in the spell if you were releasing it?"

"You are so naïve. Because I didn't release it. I thought releasing it would definitely kill him, which would have been bad news for me, with Arthur and Orlas breathing down my neck. So I just decided to re-enter it, as I have done before, and you all came too. If I had decided to recast the spell you would all be in your own prisons."

"I don't understand."

"The spell imprisons a person in his own idea of pleasure. For Merlin that is nature. He is – was – a Druid, so nature is everything to him. Here he has trees, herbs, his workshop, everything he needs to make himself happy. I even gave him his sacred grove."

She crossed to the window. "Orlas and Arthur see Merlin's prison; it is not of their own choosing, but nevertheless, they are happy here. For now. I have no idea how long that will last, as to be quite honest I have never brought anyone with me before. I wasn't even sure it would work."

Tom joined her at the window and watched them amble through the trees and around the tower.

She gazed up at him. "What sort of man are you?" Her voice had dropped to a seductive murmur. "I would like to know what prison you would be in."

As he looked down into her green eyes, he could think of nothing except how pretty she was, and his gaze drifted across her face and down to her lips. "Why do you look so young, if you're as old as Vivian?"

She laughed. "Because Vivian's appearance is an affectation. She chooses to look that way. She says it is useful to remind herself of her great age." She stepped closer to Tom, almost whispering, causing him to lean in closer to her. "I think she does it because age suggests great wisdom." Smiling conspiratorially, she added, "I prefer to have people underestimate me."

And they'd certainly done that, he thought. Annoyed with himself, he stepped back to clear his head. "Release the spell now, and then go. I won't stop you. Arthur was your friend. And he's a fair man, you know that."

She stood for some moments thinking, and then shook her head. "I can't. If I release him then I release Orlas, that damn man who bound my powers and locked me up for days."

"But how long will the spell last?" Tom asked, desperately trying to find a way out of this.

"Forever. Probably."

"People will search for us! And you. We weren't the only ones looking for you and Merlin."

"They'll have a long search."

"You know Vivian sent us here. Once she knows we've disappeared, she'll come to find us. And she'll still be looking for you! She was worried about you. Don't you care about that?"

Nimue looked absently out of the window again. "She shouldn't have bothered. She knows I can take care of myself." Abruptly she turned. "What's your name again?"

"Tom."

"Well, Tom, it's been very nice to meet you, but you've distracted me enough. I need to cast another spell to get out of here, which is, to be quite honest, long winded and difficult, and one I avoid doing if at all possible. I'm going to put you to sleep for a while so I can cast uninterrupted."

"Wait! How do we break the spell? What if we wait until you've gone?" And then he realised what she'd said. "You're going to do what to me?"

She stepped even closer to him, making him edge backwards until his back was against the wall. Pressing her fingers to his forehead, she smirked. "Don't worry, I'll be gentle."

The last thing he remembered was a feeling of overwhelming tiredness and a rising wall of blackness as he slid to the floor, unconscious.

Chapter 9 Without a Trace

Beansprout followed close behind Woodsmoke and Brenna, as Woodsmoke led the way to the cave entrance. The rain was a steady drizzle, the mist was getting thicker, and dusk was falling. She could see only a few feet in front of her.

Woodsmoke's movements were uncanny. He slipped like a ghost through the landscape; she could hardly see him. Brenna was easier to see, but silent, and Beansprout moved quickly to keep up, trying to keep her footing in the wet. For a few seconds they disappeared and she was alone, with just the shush of rain to keep her company. And then she was aware of noise – disembodied voices, shouting. She stopped, uncertain of what to do. And then Brenna and Woodsmoke reappeared, emerging wraith-like from the mist.

Woodsmoke spoke first. "Something's happened. I think I heard someone say that they've disappeared. There's a least half a dozen Cervini by the cave entrance. Wait here."

A cold feeling of dread crept through Beansprout. "Who's disappeared?"

But he'd gone.

Beansprout and Brenna looked at each other anxiously. They stood for a few minutes, listening to the muffled voices. Despite her heavy cloak, rain trickled down Beansprout's neck and caught on her eyelashes. She brushed the water away impatiently.

There was a break in the voices and she heard Woodsmoke speaking. Had they caught him? She stepped forward involuntarily, but Brenna caught her arm, gesturing at Beansprout to listen. The voices sounded calm, even reasonable. What was going on?

And then Woodsmoke appeared again. "Come on. It's all right."

He turned and led them a short distance around mounds of rock and ferns, until they emerged in front of the cave entrance where a group of Cervini stood talking. They fell silent as the three approached, and Woodsmoke said, "These are the friends I was telling you about. It's just us, and our friends you saw in the cave. We want to help."

Despite the wet and the chill, the Cervini wore only sleeveless jackets and trousers made of animal skins, and their feet were bare. There were both men and women; some had long hair, some short, and they all had curious markings on their skin.

A tall grizzled man with grey hair stepped forward. He nodded at Brenna and Beansprout and said, "Woodsmoke tells me you are friends of Arthur, the man I found in the caves." He studied Brenna for a few seconds longer and then smiled in recognition. "You are Aerikeen. Fellow shapeshifters are always welcome." Then his smile dropped. "I fear it's too late. They've disappeared and the cave is empty. They vanished before my eyes, and there was nothing I could do."

Beansprout's feeling of dread grew stronger. Surely they couldn't have just vanished? "Was Tom with him?"

"The young man? Yes, he's gone too."

"Can we see the cave?" Woodsmoke asked.

He shrugged. "If you want. Our shaman is there now. I'm Rek, the one who first recognised Nimue. I wish now I had never laid eyes on her." He sighed as he turned. "Follow me and I'll tell you what happened. If I hadn't seen it with my own eyes, I'd swear someone had made it up."

Rek led them along the winding passage, and at the cave entrance, he stopped. "This is where I was, watching it all. And there," he said, pointing to the centre of the room where a dreadlocked man stood within a circle of burning torches, "was where they were standing with Nimue. She was supposed to be releasing the spell to bring Merlin back, but the torches burned blood red and they disappeared. Gone. Then the torches went out."

Rek headed to the shaman's side. "Nerian, these are Arthur's friends, come to help."

Nerian was examining something in his hands, but he looked up, his dark eyes bleak. "Your help is welcome, but if I'm honest, I'm not sure what we can do. I've been trying to work out what Nimue has done. These are the herbs she used - the remains of those herbs she left at the entrance."

"May I?" asked Woodsmoke, holding out his hands.

Nerian handed them over. "I recognise wormwood, sage and vervain, but there is something else in there I'm not familiar with."

Woodsmoke sniffed the bundle and wrinkled his nose. "It's bitter."

"Yes, I'll work it out," Nerian said.

"You didn't know the spell, I presume?"

"No. If I'd realised what was happening, I'd have stopped her." He looked around the cave. "There is nothing else here to help."

"Could you repeat the spell, if we had the herbs?" Brenna asked.

He shook his head, uncertain. "I don't think so. I couldn't hear what she was saying. She was very careful to remain quiet."

Brenna exchanged a worried glance with Woodsmoke. "Do you mind if we look around?"

"Go ahead."

Brenna changed form and flew up and around the cave, while Beansprout joined Woodsmoke as he paced around, grim faced and irritable.

"What are we looking for?" she asked him. The cave was uniformly bare; the floor a mixture of rock and earth, and moisture trickled down the rock walls.

"I honestly have no idea. Something that looks like it doesn't belong here I suppose." He paused, struggling to contain his temper. "I *knew* something like this would happen! Arthur should have waited."

"But even if we'd been here, we couldn't have stopped this. We'd have either disappeared with them, or watched them, like Rek did. At least we're able to help now."

Woodsmoke just grunted.

They continued their search, but the cave yielded nothing; whatever was here had been hidden very well. They returned to the Nerian and Rek who were deep in hushed conversation.

"This is hopeless," Woodsmoke said to them. "We can't find anything! Brenna?"

She shook her head. "Nothing, sorry."

Panic had started its insidious spread through Beansprout. "Nerian, I know you can't do Nimue's spell, but can you break it?"

"Usually only the witch who cast it can break it," he said. "Unless death intervenes. But I've had an idea. I'm going to summon Herne."

"Who's that?" asked Beansprout.

"The God of the wilds, the moors, the forests, the ancient rocks; his magic is earthy and powerful. It is rumoured that Merlin was like a child to him. I feel sure he will release him."

Woodsmoke frowned. "Surely he would have released Merlin a lot sooner than now?"

"But we never knew what had really happened to Merlin before. And besides," Nerian said, sounding slightly offended, "Gods do not usually intervene in our affairs."

"And we summon him how?" asked Brenna, ever practical.

"Here, where the spell has been worked. But first I must return to the Great Hall, there are things I need to collect for the ritual. And we must tell the others what has happened. I'll be back within a day."

Woodsmoke nodded his agreement. "I'll go and fetch the horses and we'll sleep in the first cave tonight. At least we'll be dry."

As the others made their way out of the cave, Beansprout paused within the circle of burning torches. Whatever magic Nimue had used was impressive, and Beansprout had a thrill of excitement as she realised what she wanted to do with her new life in the Other.

She was going to learn magic.

Chapter 10 Spells and Potions

When Tom woke up he had no idea how long he'd been unconscious for. The first things he became aware of were the cold, dusty floorboards pressed against his face, and the soreness of his right arm trapped beneath him. He rolled over onto his back, flexed his arm gently, and then sat up, wondering what had happened.

Nimue had gone, but other than that, the room looked the same. Had she really left them here? He struggled to his feet, shouting, "Nimue!" over and over again. But his calls were swallowed by the walls, and the silence quickly settled round him.

What was he going to do? If he did nothing he would be trapped here with the others, possibly forever, and he was in the unenviable position of being fully aware he was trapped in a spell. He'd go mad. There was no delirious enchantment to muffle his mind. He paused for a moment, weighing up his options. His unease doubled as he stood alone, feeling the weight of eons shifting around him. It was as if he was suffocating.

Suddenly it struck him – he knew what his talisman was. The silver bough, tucked in a pocket of his cloak. Fahey had said something about it protecting him. But from what? Madness? And then he had a moment of panic; had Nimue stolen it while he was unconscious? He patted his pocket and sighed with relief. It was still there. How come it didn't protect him from specific spells? He shrugged. He had enough to worry about.

He turned to Merlin. Perhaps if he could rouse him, Merlin might be able get them out. But then he realised – if Merlin could do that, surely he would have escaped years ago.

The advantage of not being enchanted, like the others, was that he had his sanity, and a talisman. Tom straightened his shoulders with determination. He was going to get them out of there.

First things first, he couldn't just leave Merlin lying on the floor. It was wrong. He ran downstairs and grabbed a pillow and blankets off the bed, putting the pillow under Merlin's head and wrapping the blankets around him. It was probably pointless, but it made Tom feel better.

Now it was time to see how Arthur and Orlas were. Outside the tower the air was mild, with hardly a breath of wind. It felt like spring or autumn, as if it was the beginning or the end of something, but some trees were in full leaf, while others were shedding leaves – layers of their rich reds and russets were strewn across the ground, collecting in bundles against jumbles of rocks and in overgrown thickets. Daffodils nodded in the sunshine, and a tangle of roses was growing through the trees. Tom was sure all this wasn't meant to happen at the same time. If this place had no seasons, did it also mean it had no day or night? He would soon find out. But that also filled him with panic. How would he know how long they had been there? The Other already had a misplaced sense of time; with no markers at all he could be here centuries and never know. What if he'd been here months already?

But it felt almost beyond time, with a watchfulness that could wait, and had waited, for millennia. He was tempted to see if there was a boundary, and was about to set off in a straight line, keeping the tower behind him, when he decided against it. There was a very real chance he could get lost, or even forget what he was doing in the first place. Which was? Oh yes. Getting out of here. He shook himself. Was he drugged? He had to act. Now. Before he fell asleep, like Merlin.

He could see Arthur the bear, absently wandering through the trees. He made a beeline for him, jumping over streams and scrambling over boulders, before coming to a halt a short distance away. Feeling foolish, he shouted, "Arthur, can you hear me? See me? Hello! Are you in there?" But the bear simply shook himself like a gigantic dog and ignored him. And Orlas, grazing in the distance, continued to tear up huge chunks of grass. Whatever Tom decided to do, he was going to be doing it alone.

He raced back to Merlin's room. If Merlin had taught Nimue the spell, and if the tower was a representation of Merlin's workshop, then the spell must be here somewhere, maybe in a spell book. And if he found it, he might find a way to reverse it.

He was worried that something in the room might have changed, but he found it just as he had left it. The fire still burned, and candles still spluttered in dark nooks. He doubted Merlin's spell book would be on one of the shelves; surely it would be on a workbench if he used it frequently. He started looking on the bench furthest from the door. Papers were scattered across it haphazardly, and he rifled through them. What did a spell book look like? Old and leather-bound? He found letters, scrawled notes, books on animals, birds, and the properties of stones. But no spell book.

He moved on to the middle bench, working methodically from one end to the other, getting distracted by drawings of eyes, dissected hearts, and other grisly organs. And then, buried beneath a pile of papers and bags of herbs, he found it. A huge, black, leather-bound book of spells.

He cleared the space around it, and opened it carefully. It was very old, and worn with use. The front cover was marked and stained, and when he opened it he found the spine was broken, and the pages turned easily, some loose at the edges. The pages were well worn too, the edges grubby where they had been handled.

A quick glance was enough to show him there were hundreds of spells. Each started on a new page, and some were long, going on for pages, while others were only a few lines. There were notes and small drawings in the margins, and trapped within some pages were feathers, herbs or flowers, and what looked like fragments of animal skins. The writing was small and cramped, as if spiders had walked through ink and scrambled across the page.

Tom sighed. This could take a while. He pulled over a stool and settled in.

After what seemed like hours, during which he became distracted by several bizarre-sounding spells, Tom eventually reached the end of the book. There was no spell for imprisoning a person. That made sense – why would Merlin want to write that down?

A wave of despair washed over him and he realised he was very tired. How could he break a spell he couldn't even find? He rubbed his face and put his head in his hands. He had never felt so lonely. His eyes were closing with tiredness, and he rested his head on the spell book, his head spinning with questions.

Seconds later, he jerked upright. Nimue hadn't recast this spell, she had just taken them back into it. That was a different spell. He needed to reverse Nimue's spell, so that should be the spell he looked for. Now he groaned again. If he was to rescue Merlin, he would have to find the original spell and reverse that. But by reversing the spell and rescuing them, would he kill Merlin? Nimue had thought so.

His head hurt. Magic was complicated, and he had no idea what to do.

He dragged himself to his feet. He had to find the spell to imprison a person. It had to be here somewhere. Damn Nimue. And damn her green eyes.

Chapter 11 Merlin's Cave

Beansprout sat in a circle with Brenna, Woodsmoke and about a dozen Cervini, in what they had now named Merlin's Cave.

Nerian had returned earlier that afternoon with small drums, herbs, and what looked like ceremonial clothing. He had arrived in stag form, with everything attached by a harness to his back. When he turned back to human form the harness hung from his shoulders and he was almost bowed beneath the weight of his pack. He had immediately summoned all of the Cervini, leaving only a few to guard the entrance as a precaution.

Beansprout felt oddly claustrophobic. When she'd stepped onto the moor that morning, the rain had stopped, but with the granite walls rearing up behind her, and the mist pressing in thickly from all sides, the world seemed to have become very small and ominous. And now that so many of them were crowded into the cave, it felt much smaller than it had done when she'd first entered it yesterday.

She admitted to herself that she felt a little scared. She was about to participate in a ceremony to summon Herne. A God. Nerian had stressed that he needed as many people as possible, because it raised the energy levels. Part of her expected absolutely nothing to happen; that it would be a ceremony of words and gesticulations only. But the other part of her thought something would happen, because this was the Other, a place of magic and strange creatures, where the laws of reality were reversed. And she wanted to experience that more deeply than ever. And of course, she wanted Tom and Arthur to return.

The ground was cold, and she sat on a folded blanket, her cloak pulled around her. Woodsmoke was to her right, with Brenna next to him. A young female Cervini sat to her left. The Cervini seemed impervious to the cold, sitting cross-legged on the bare earth, patiently waiting for the ceremony to begin.

Beansprout turned to Woodsmoke and whispered, "Have you done this before?"

"No, but I've heard about such ceremonies. They can be quite long. Are you all right? You don't have to join in."

"Yes, I'm fine. Just curious. Do you think he'll come? That Nerian will actually summon a god?"

"Let's hope so. Gods are stubborn beings."

Nerian had lit a small fire in the centre of the cave, the smoke drifting up into the unseen heights. He sat next to it, bare-chested, wearing an elaborate headdress of antlers and a necklace of feathers and bones, his appearance grotesque in the flickering light. Next to him he'd arranged various items, and something bright glinted in the pale light. It had a familiar shape, and Beansprout squirmed in her seat trying to get a better view. It looked like Tom's silver branch, but a little bigger.

Satisfied the fire was burning as he needed it, Nerian gestured to the circle. When the steady beat of drums started, he dropped a bunch of herbs into the flames. Beating another rhythm on his own small skin drum, he began to chant. The effect was hypnotic. Very quickly, Beansprout lost all track of time and settled in, mesmerised.

Chapter 12 Insidious Spells

Tom had found a shelf filled with very old books – and that was saying something, considering everything here looked ancient. They were high, out of reach, and tucked to the back of the shelf, so it was quite by chance that he saw them. Were they hidden for a reason? He pulled a stool over and stepped onto it, clutching the shelves for support.

One of the books drew his gaze immediately. It had a deep green leather cover and was unembellished, except for an image of bound hands. He reached for the book, and as soon as he touched it he felt a tingle in his fingers, so much so that he nearly dropped it. Did he just imagine that? It had felt like an electric shock.

He reached forward again, preparing himself for another jolt, but this time felt only a residual hum, as if it was vibrating in his hands. Breathing deeply to steady himself, he opened the book. Most of the pages were blank, but the half a dozen or so spells it did contain were spells of imprisonment. There were spells to lock the tongue, to bind the mind to a single moment, to bind within the form of an animal, to imprison within rocks or trees, to imprison within a nightmare, and … to imprison a person. Tom's heart raced and his mouth became dry as he realised he'd found it. But he still needed to know how to reverse it.

He put the book down and looked at the others it was shelved with. There was a book of poisons, one of blood rites and sacrifices which looked particularly gruesome, and then a thin ragged-edged book with a white cover, which had no markings on at all. Opening it, he found it contained one long spell: The spell of reversal for all spells worked under the sun and moon, by fire or blood, and in which the will is bound by insidious means. There was a warning next to it: Only to be used in times of direst need as reversal of a spell cast by another involves the release of potent energies which can be fatal.

Great. The spell that might release him could kill him. And Merlin. And maybe the others.

The spell of reversal stressed that specific ingredients from the original spell must be used. Scanning through both spells, he found a list of the things he needed, but both specified that it was important to cast the spell in a place of power, such as in a grove of sacred trees. Now that did sound familiar. Nimue had said there was one here. Looking out of the tower windows, he saw a small circle of trees, in the centre of which was a flat rock and blackened fire pit. That would do. Now he needed to find everything else.

Almost an hour later, Tom sat within the circle of trees, a small fire burning in front of him. There were bowls of herbs within easy reach, and in one there was also a cutting of Merlin's hair and a clipping of his nails. Tom reached into his pocket and took out his silver branch, resting it in his lap. His heart pounding, he double- and triple-checked everything, then started the spell. Whether he messed this up or got it right, he could easily die.

Chapter 13 The Summoning

Beansprout felt disembodied as the smoke drifted through the cave, and the circle became indistinct. Nerian sat immobile by the fire, his drum on the floor in front of him. Strange shadows cast by the flames made his face appear to change shape, morphing into someone, or something else. Time had lost all meaning, and she was aware of only the drumming, her heartbeat, her breath, and the fire flickering in the centre of the room.

Then Nerian threw his head back and howled. The sound was so unearthly and unexpected that shivers rippled across her skin, the sound reaching into her very being until it seemed she was howling too. But she couldn't move and couldn't speak, and she couldn't take her eyes off Nerian.

Nerian wasn't Nerian any more. He seemed to have swelled in size, becoming huge and imposing, his chest strong and muscled, and the antlers large and many tined. His eyes were black, and he looked slowly around the room, his gaze raking through her. A scene imposed itself over the cave, flickering in and out of focus ... a grove of tall trees, mossy grass, and lichen-covered boulders, and beyond them a glinting silver tower.

Beansprout saw Tom, sitting on the far side of the fire, looking small in such an ancient place. Whatever Nerian had become stood and gazed towards the silver tower and howled again and again, until she thought she would go mad or deaf. Then he strode around the fire and reached out to Tom.

There was an enormous booming sound as if the earth itself had shattered.

The fire flared brilliantly into a column of flame, shooting high into the cave, and with another wild keening that seemed to come from all directions, a fierce wind carrying the dust of a thousand years ran through the cave, whipping Beansprout's hair around her face and into her mouth, and she covered her eyes until it had passed. Then the fire shrank to the smallest pin-prick of light. The cave now felt as if it encompassed a universe, and the fire was the sun that burnt a galaxy away. Beansprout felt tiny, lost in the void, and she tipped forward, dizzy and terrified, having lost all sense of who and where she was; and then it was over.

The cave was just a cave again and the fire had returned to normal. Sprawled unconscious in a heap by the fire, was Nerian, and next to him were the inert bodies of Tom, Arthur, Orlas, and an old man with a long white beard.

Beansprout wasn't quite sure of the order of what happened next, but after seconds in which everyone seemed to be in a state of immovable shock, Woodsmoke and two of the Cervini recovered and ran to the bodies in the centre of the room. Woodsmoke crouched beside Tom and then Arthur, and one of the Cervini checked Orlas, and with relief they shouted that they were still alive.

And then Rek spoke. "Merlin is dead."

A sigh swept around the room as the news sank in. Beansprout stood on weak legs that protested beneath her – how long had she been sitting? – and made her way to the centre of the room. The Cervini crouched around Merlin, touching his hands and hair.

Beansprout was curious to see Merlin, but was more worried about Tom and Arthur. A chill seemed to have descended as the fire burned low. She threw some logs on and prodded it into life, then gathered some blankets and with Brenna and Woodsmoke's help, wrapped the unconscious bodies to keep them warm.

Arthur, Orlas and Tom were pale and clammy, their breathing shallow. The strange markings on Orlas's skin stood out against his pallor, making his otherness more apparent. It seemed they were only just clinging to life.

"Do you think they'll be OK?" she asked Brenna.

"I don't know. But they're strong. I'm sure it will just take a while," she answered, but her expression did not carry the conviction of her words.

A groan disturbed Beansprout's thoughts, and next to her Nerian stirred back to life.

Rek moved quickly to his side. "Nerian, it's Rek. Can you hear me?"

Nerian mumbled something and blinked rapidly, and in a few seconds his confusion cleared and he muttered hoarsely, "Did it work?"

Rek smiled thinly. "Well you summoned Herne and broke the spell."

Nerian groaned again. "I know I summoned Herne! That's why my head pounds!" He closed his eyes as if to shut out bad news. "And I know Merlin's dead. The others?"

"Alive. But only just."

Nerian opened his eyes again, looking more hopeful. "Good! Help me sit up."

Rek lifted him, putting an arm behind him to support his shoulders, and offered Nerian a warm smoky drink that smelt of peat fires.

After a few mouthfuls Nerian said, "That was a strong spell. It's a wonder they weren't all killed. I think Tom's attempt to break the spell helped."

"Tom did what?" Beansprout asked, confused.

"He was trying to break the spell. I saw him, through Herne, as we crossed between the real and the illusion."

Woodsmoke smiled. "Really? Very enterprising."

"Herne has given me instructions." Nerian paused and looked at Rek. "When we have recovered, we go to Ceridwen's Cauldron."

"We do what?" Rek spluttered.

Nerian looked bemused. "Surprising, yes?"

"But no one has been there for years!"

Beansprout interrupted. "Will someone please tell me what that is?" She turned to Woodsmoke and Brenna. "Have you heard of this cauldron place?"

They shook their heads, equally confused.

Nerian's eyes glittered in the firelight. "It is an ancient place. A place of rebirth. The place where we bring Merlin back to life."

Beansprout thought she must have misunderstood. *Bring Merlin back to life?*

Rek sounded nervous. "It is forbidden ground."

"Forbidden by Herne. And now it is not. I told you he would do anything for Merlin."

Woodsmoke and Beansprout looked out across the moors. Dawn was breaking and a sliver of pale green light illuminated the horizon. The rain and heavy mist of the previous days had rolled away, revealing a sodden landscape pockmarked with pools and streams. And it was cold. Beansprout pulled her cloak close around her shoulders.

"Just when I think I'm getting use to this place, I find out something new, and it leaves me feeling weird again."

Woodsmoke smiled. "The trick is to never presume too much here."

"I suppose so," she sighed, "but I'm worried about this Cauldron place. It sounds dangerous."

"Well at least Tom and Arthur won't need it."

"But they're not awake yet."

"No. But they're not dead. And we'll be leaving for the Great Hall later. They'll be better cared for there. It will be warmer than a cave, at least."

"What happens after Merlin's resurrection – if it works?"

Woodsmoke shrugged. "Maybe we look for Nimue. Maybe we go home."

Beansprout frowned. Part of her was desperate to meet the witch with the amazing magic, but the other part of her was worried. "What's the point in looking for her? She'll be hiding somewhere. Or even if she's not, what could we do? She might put a spell on us."

"I guess it depends on how vengeful Arthur is."

"I thought you were annoyed with Arthur?"

Woodsmoke stared absently over the moors. "I am. But I'm not about to let him run off with Tom again."

"But Tom isn't a child. If he wants to go with Arthur we can't stop him. He might be feeling pretty vengeful himself."

It took a couple of days travel to reach the White Woods. Some of the Cervini were harnessed to a large cart carrying Merlin and the unconscious bodies of the others. They pulled it along at a funereal pace, and Beansprout was tired by the time they arrived.

The White Woods were named for the ghostly white trees that grew there. Their tall, spindly trunks stretched high above their heads, the leaves turning from a pale green to red in the autumn weather.

A large group of Cervini in human form greeted them at the main door of the Great Hall, a solid single-storied building made from the pale wood that surrounded them. Half a dozen Cervini lifted the lifeless body of Merlin onto a pallet and carried him into the recesses of the hall, while Orlas was moved with equal ceremony to his chambers. Tom and Arthur were carried to a room for the sick, and once they were tended to, Rek led Beansprout, Brenna, and Woodsmoke to a series of interlinked rooms with simple beds and rugs.

"I'll make sure you have food bought to you later," he told them. "And I'll let you know when we have planned the ceremony at the Cauldron. Rest while you can. In case you hadn't realised, you're coming too."

Chapter 14 The White Woods

As Tom drifted into consciousness he became aware of a pale light flickering beyond his closed eyes, and a splitting headache. The weight of blankets pressed against his stiff limbs. He opened his eyes and squinted against the light, edging himself to a sitting position. That was a mistake. His headache got worse and he was violently sick on the floor next to his bed. He collapsed back onto the bed and passed out.

Several hours later he woke up again. His headache had now subsided to a dull thump, his stomach felt horribly empty, and his mouth felt like sandpaper. He cautiously looked round the room, careful not to move too much. It was dim; a candle burned on the table next to him, beside a jug of water and a glass. Overhead he could make out the wooden beams of the low ceiling.

He really needed some water. Slowly he sat up and leaned back against plump pillows, taking a few steadying breaths. Where the hell was he? He remembered sitting next to a fire in a grove of trees and seeing a tall powerful man with huge antlers striding across the clearing towards him, and then nothing. Blackness.

He poured himself a glass of water and sipped slowly, his throat painfully dry. A fire burned in a stone fireplace, the only source of light other than the flickering candle. It showed a small room with half a dozen wooden-framed beds in it, and one long narrow window high in the wall opposite him. It was dark outside. Arthur lay in the bed next to him, still sleeping.

None of this explained where he was or how he had got here. But as he was wondering what to do, the door opened and a young male Cervini appeared. He smiled when he saw Tom sitting.

"You're awake. Good. I'll fetch Nerian. Do you need anything before I go?"

Tom shook his head, bewildered, and croaked, "No."

A few minutes later the dreadlocked shaman appeared.

"You survived then," Nerian said as he walked over to Tom. "Remember me?"

Tom nodded. "Vaguely."

"How are you feeling?"

"Terrible. My head aches and my throat hurts. Where am I?"

Nerian sat on a chair next to the bed. "In the Great Hall of the Cervini. Your friends are here too. You're lucky you only have a bad head. Do you remember what happened?"

"I remember sitting by a fire in a grove of trees, but I don't know why I was there."

"What's the last thing you remember?"

Tom realised he couldn't remember much of anything. "I remember the cave, and Nimue started the spell, and then nothing. Nothing at all until the antlered man."

"You remember Herne?" Nerian looked surprised. "Don't worry, hopefully your memories will return in time. The spell Nimue cast was powerful, and when it broke it nearly killed you all. It did kill Merlin."

"Oh, Merlin. I'd forgotten about him." Tom clutched his head again as the headache started to return.

"That's OK Tom, enough now. I'll bring you a drink that will help, and then I want to you to rest again."

When Tom next woke it was morning, and Arthur was awake in the bed next to him.

"About time! Get up lazy bones!"

Tom groaned as he sat up. "Funny aren't you, Arthur?"

Arthur's face was ashen, and his long dark hair looked wild and unkempt. He leaned back on a mound of pillows and gazed wearily at Tom. "I'm trying to find humour in our situation."

"Mmm. Keep trying. I feel half dead."

"I know that feeling. This is better than that. But from what Nerian said, we almost died. Merlin did, you know." Arthur gazed into space, his mind clearly elsewhere.

"I know. I'm sorry." Tom plumped up his pillows and leaned back. "Can you remember anything? I can remember flashes of things. Nimue, a silver tower, lots of trees."

"More than me. It seems like a dream. All I can see is trees, trees and more trees. I feel like I'm drunk just thinking about it. I didn't even see Merlin. To be so close ..." His voice was full of an aching regret.

"There was nothing you could have done, Arthur," Tom said, trying to console his friend. To distract him, he asked, "How long were we unconscious?" And then another thought struck him and he sat up straighter. "How long were we in the spell?"

"Not long, fortunately. These Cervini work quickly. About a day in the spell, and three days unconscious."

"Wow. Four days lost. Better than four years, I suppose. Or more." He paused, contemplating their possible fate and lucky escape. Memories now started to trickle back, of their time in the spell and their deliberate abandonment by Nimue. He looked at Arthur, horror spreading across his face. "What were we thinking, Arthur? We should have known better." He felt sick at the thought of how long they could have been trapped.

Arthur looked at him sharply and if anything, turned paler. "Tom, I should–"

The door opened, interrupting their conversation, and Beansprout entered. She smiled, relief evident on her face. "You're both awake! Nerian said you were OK."

"Just about," Arthur grumbled.

She plonked herself on the end of Tom's bed. "Tell me everything!"

"Only if you tell us what we're doing here," Tom said.

"You're recovering! We're preparing to go to Ceridwen's Cauldron to resurrect Merlin."

Arthur sat bolt upright. "Where? To that old hag? To do what?"

"Steady on, Arthur," Beansprout joked. "What old hag?"

"Ceridwen. How can she even still be alive?"

"I don't know what you're talking about," Beansprout said, looking at Arthur curiously. "I think you're still delirious. Ceridwen's Cauldron is a place, not a person. It's a hidden and forbidden place where someone can be resurrected from the dead."

"Well she was a hag when I was alive!" Arthur railed. "But – you said we're resurrecting Merlin?"

Tom, also confused, stared at Beansprout.

Beansprout looked surprised. "You didn't know? Nerian didn't tell you?"

"I can't believe it!" Arthur looked awestruck. "I'll see Merlin again, and you'll get to meet him." His excitement quickly vanished, and he gazed into space. "I can't believe that Nimue trapped him for all those years ..."

Arthur fell into a brooding silence, and Beansprout looked worriedly at him before turning to Tom. She curled up at the end of the bed, making herself comfortable. "Spill then, Tom. What happened to you?"

Later that day, when Nerian was satisfied that Tom and Arthur were recovered, Beansprout showed them to their rooms.

Tom still felt tired and his limbs were weak, but after a long talk with everyone he was finally able to piece together the events of the past few days. His memories of their time inside the spell had now returned, but he found it difficult to believe how real it had all felt.

The one memory he couldn't shake was that of Nimue's green eyes. No matter how hard he tried to banish them from his mind, they kept returning, taunting him.

"You all right, Tom?" Woodsmoke asked. "You look miles away."

With a jerk Tom turned. "Yes, fine."

They were seated on thick cushions around a small low table, while Brenna updated them on the latest plans.

"Ceridwen's Cauldron is higher on the moors than Scar Face Fell. It's a lonely place, apparently, deserted now, and a few days' travel from here in a place called Enisled. Ceridwen was a real person, and her cauldron had the power of rebirth,

93

inspiration and knowledge. When she died, the place was sealed. Access to the cauldron has been blocked for centuries."

Arthur interrupted. "There you go. I knew I recognised the name!"

"Why was it sealed?" Beansprout asked.

Woodsmoke answered. "It wouldn't do, would it, to keep resurrecting anyone who died?"

"No, I suppose not," she said. "It sort of makes a mockery of death."

Arthur squirmed uncomfortably in his seat. "Like me you mean?"

"No, of course not!" Beansprout said aghast. "Your rebirth was a deal, arranged by Merlin for Vivian. Neither he nor you had any choice."

"And yet you seem to treat it so lightly, Arthur," Woodsmoke said with a grim look, "and the lives of those around you."

A silence fell around the table as Arthur looked stonily back at him. "I do not treat it lightly. Or the lives of others. But I am sorry about what happened at the Fell. I said I'd wait and I didn't. I got carried away."

Woodsmoke glared at him. "Yes you did. You nearly killed both of you."

"Sometimes decisions have to be made in very little time," Arthur spat. "I was worried that if we didn't act quickly, we'd never know what had happened to Merlin. However, the consequences were greater than I thought." He turned to Tom. "I'm sorry, Tom. I put you in a difficult position."

Tom looked uncomfortable and stuttered, "It's OK Arthur."

Woodsmoke persisted. "No, it's not OK. Does Vivian know about any of this? She said she'd be in touch after the Meet."

"No, I haven't heard from her since before then."

"So Vivian doesn't know about Merlin and the spell, or Nimue's part in it?"

"Not from me." Arthur looked thoughtfully at Woodsmoke. "Unless she saw it all by scrying?"

"It seems strange she hasn't been in touch when she was so anxious to keep track of our progress."

They fell into an uneasy silence as they realised Woodsmoke was right. They had been so caught up in the chase they had almost forgotten about Vivian.

"Have we heard how Orlas is?" Woodsmoke asked Brenna.

"He's fine. He woke at the same time as Arthur and Tom. He'll be travelling with us. We're going to wait another day or two for him to fully recover, and then we leave."

"So we're all going?" Tom asked.

"Yes. Herne's instructions. It's thanks to our involvement – particularly your efforts, Tom – that the spell was broken, so we are to join the resurrection."

"It was mainly self-preservation. I didn't want to be stuck in that spell forever. And frankly, Arthur," Tom joked, trying to lighten the atmosphere, "you weren't much help. You were a bear."

"A bear? And you've only just thought to tell me? No wonder all I can remember is trees!" he exclaimed.

"Sorry, I've had a lot on my mind. Nimue said it was your animal spirit."

Brenna laughed, "You'll be shapeshifting with me soon."

"You still have the silver branch, Tom?" Beansprout asked.

He patted his pocket. "It never leaves me."

"And what are we doing about Nimue?" Arthur asked.

"I don't give a damn about Nimue," Woodsmoke said. "We should leave her be."

Brenna and Beansprout agreed, Brenna adding, "She's dangerous, and the spell's broken. What's the point? She's lived quietly since she first put Merlin in the spell, and she's probably returned to Vivian, or carried on to Raghnall. Perhaps that's why Vivian hasn't been in touch."

Arthur didn't answer, nodding slowly and staring at the table again.

Brenna exchanged a glance with Woodsmoke and then added gently, almost persuasively, "We have Merlin. There is nothing else to gain, Arthur. And Vivian was worried about Nimue's welfare. Now that we know she was, and is, deliberately hiding, your obligation is over."

He gave a brief nod. "Well, I need to stretch my legs." And without further comment he left the room, leaving the others looking worriedly at each other.

"I don't think Arthur can leave this," Tom said. "He might feel guilty about almost getting us killed, but I think his need to find Nimue is greater."

Woodsmoke looked grim. "Revenge is not our problem, Tom. And it is most definitely not your problem."

And while Tom knew this, he also knew that it wasn't that simple.

Chapter 15 Risky Business

The following morning, Tom stayed inside the Great Hall, which meant doing a lot of eating as well as sleeping. The others decided to explore the White Woods, apart from Arthur, who sat alone in the cellars with Merlin's body. He seemed mired in indecision and guilt, and Tom wasn't sure how to get him out of his strange mood.

Later, they were summoned to Orlas's private rooms, following a servant down the long corridors into the rear of the building. Arthur trailed behind, silent and morose.

The servant knocked on a door and ushered them through. Orlas stood in the middle of the room, leaning on a large wooden table. In front of him was a map, which he was studying with great concentration. Tom had almost forgotten what Orlas looked like, their first meeting had been so brief. His dark hair hung loose around his shoulders, and his arms were bare, his stag markings looking like tattoos against his skin. Thick gold torcs were wrapped around the tops of both arms and his neck. A young woman stood next to him. She had long red hair, and her skin glowed with pale red Cervini markings. She too had a gold torc wrapped around each arm.

It took the pair a few seconds to register their arrival, then they strode across the room to greet them. Orlas shook their hands, his grip firm and reassuring.

"Arthur, Tom. It's good to see you again and a pleasure to meet the rest of you. Let me introduce you to Aislin, my wife."

She stepped forward. "Welcome to the Great Hall. I'm sorry I haven't met you sooner." She glanced at Orlas. "I've been pre-occupied."

"Understandably," Brenna said, reassuring her.

Aislin smiled at her warmly. "It's been a worrying few days, hasn't it? Come, have a seat and we can talk properly."

She led them to chairs grouped around the fire, and when they were settled, Orlas turned to Tom and Arthur. "I trust you have recovered?"

Arthur nodded. "More or less. How are you?"

"The same, although I gather we're lucky to be alive."

"You helped break the spell," Aislin said to Tom.

"So everyone keeps saying," Tom said, still bewildered by the whole event. "But I'm not sure I really helped. I wasn't sure anything in there was real enough to work."

"Nerian disagrees. Anyway, you're here – despite Nimue's best intentions." A flush of anger coloured Aislin's pale face.

It seemed Beansprout was also confused by Tom's time in the spell. "So even though the spell was a powerful illusion, the things in it were real? I mean, they could be used?"

"You are asking things that are beyond my knowledge," Orlas answered. "I reverted to my stag form, and was so completely in the spell I saw only endless woods. But Tom," Orlas leaned forward, staring at Tom with his dark brown eyes, "you spent time with Nimue. Where did she go?"

"I have no idea. She said she was going to cast another spell to escape, and made me unconscious so that I wouldn't interfere."

"She gave no clue? Think carefully."

Tom shook his head. He'd been racking his brains about it since waking. "Nothing."

"Do you think she has returned to Vivian, or Raghnall?"

"I doubt either of them. When I said Vivian would still be worried about her, she didn't care. She said she could look after herself."

Orlas looked frustrated and Arthur asked, "Do you want to find her?"

"Not really. But I want to know what she's up to. You knew her well, Arthur. What do you think she'll do?"

"No idea. But I know she's determined and confident. She stepped into Merlin's place in court as if she'd been there for years."

Woodsmoke intervened. "I really don't think finding her would achieve anything, Orlas," he said, repeating his earlier argument. Tom saw Arthur bristle, but he remained silent, looking only at Orlas.

Orlas sighed. "I agree. In fact I hope she's a long way from here. We should concentrate on the things we can fix. Like Merlin."

Arthur's shoulders drooped in disappointment and he stared into the fire.

Aislin spoke, her gaze falling on them one by one, weighing their response. "I disagree with Orlas about resurrecting Merlin. He was a friend to us, a great friend, but nevertheless I think we are interfering with things that should be left well alone." Orlas went to interrupt, but she stilled him with her hand. "I know it is Herne's will. It doesn't mean

I like it. You have risked your life once for Merlin. I don't think you should risk it again." She looked towards the door at the rear of the room, from where they could hear children laughing.

Orlas rested his hand gently on hers. "We will be fine." To the others, "Are you well enough to travel?"

They nodded.

"Good. We'll leave tomorrow for Enisled."

That night the Cervini held a banquet for those travelling with Merlin. The main meeting hall was decorated with cut branches, the green and red leaves bright against the pale wooden walls. Fresh rushes were strewn across the floor releasing their sweet scent into the air, and lanterns lined the walls and hung from the ceiling, casting a soft glow over the room. The tables were crowded with steaming bowls of food, and beer and wine were flowing. The Cervini were packed into the hall, and jostled together, elbow to elbow, good natured and excited at the prospect of Merlin's return.

Tom found himself seated next to an old frail Cervini who creaked when he moved. He looked as if once he sat down, he'd never be able to stand again. He proved, however, to have the most enormous appetite, and took the opportunity to fill his bowl and his cup many times. He introduced himself as Wulfsige, and he cocked a sly eye at Tom over his beer.

"So you got trapped by the beautiful Nimue, did you?"

Tom was about to protest, then laughed. "Yes. Unfortunately I did."

"Devious, isn't she?" he smirked, ripping bread with his fingers and mopping up his stew.

Tom turned, suddenly attentive. "You know her?"

"Knew her. I haven't seen her for a very long time. I thought the witch was going to kill me."

Tom looked at him and wondered if he was joking. "Why would she do that?"

Wulfsige smiled, his face dissolving into a thousand wrinkles. "I was a young man then. A hunter. One of the best. I tracked wolves. And I was tracking wolves that day …" He looked across the room as if he could still see them. "I caught her in the woods with Merlin. She was hypnotising him, or something like that. Beneath a withered tree." He became serious. "She turned on me with such fury I thought that was the end of me. Those eyes. They were glowing."

Immediately Nimue's green eyes were back again, filling Tom's vision. Wulfsige watched him. "They grab you, don't they, Tom? Fill your brain until you can see only them."

Tom blinked and nodded, his throat suddenly dry. He took a slug of beer.

"That might have been it for me, but for my hunting hound, Nyra. She'd been ranging ahead, but she suddenly burst in from the undergrowth, howling as if a great demon from the Fire Realm was chasing her. She completely distracted Nimue, and then Merlin stirred, and I grabbed her by the scruff of her neck and ran. I don't think we stopped running 'til we reached the moors." Wulfsige refilled his bowl and started eating again.

"What happened then? Did she ever find you?" Tom asked.

"I don't think she got a good look at me. And I extended my hunt for a few days, just to make sure I avoided her."

"So what do you think she was doing?"

"Nothing good." He looked up from his bowl. "You take care. She's had a quiet few years, but don't let that fool you."

"Surely it's only Merlin she had a problem with. She helped Arthur for ages after Merlin disappeared."

"It didn't stop her the other day though, did it?" he said wryly.

Tom took another long drink and wondered why Nimue hadn't taken his talisman when she had the chance. Was it because she couldn't, because Vivian had given it to him? Or was it something else? Did she want them to have a chance? He shook his head. Woodsmoke was right. They should keep well away from Nimue.

Chapter 16 Enisled

Enisled appeared ahead of them, swathed in mist; a collection of eroded rock faces rising out of the wind-blown heather. Rek led their group along an old disused track that led across a land of windswept grass, small pools and tumbled rocks. He was followed by Orlas and Nerian, two Cervini pulling Merlin's body along in a covered cart, and another four Cervini who had come for support – huge beasts with broad shoulders and many tined antlers. All the Cervini travelled in stag form. Tom and the others were behind, travelling on horseback.

As they drew closer, it became clear that the eroded rocks were in fact a castle, ravaged by time and the elements. The track led them to a choked archway of stones and earth, on either side of which was a surprisingly solid perimeter wall.

The Cervini changed form, securing the cart containing Merlin's body, while Nerian examined the archway.

"What are you looking for?" Tom asked, puzzled.

"The key to the spell protecting the cauldron," Rek explained, as Nerian was too distracted to reply.

"Didn't Herne remove it?"

"No. But he told Nerian how to."

"Ha!" Nerian scoffed. "In theory."

Seeing them watching him, Nerian waved them away. "Give me space. This could take a while."

Arthur's mood seemed to have improved now they were on the move again, and he urged his horse to the left. "Come on. Let's check the perimeter while we wait."

"So you knew Ceridwen, Arthur?" Beansprout asked, as she rode alongside him, Tom close behind.

"Not really. I met her once. But she had quite the reputation."

"Why?"

"She was powerful and independent, and refused to be allied to anyone. But that was fine. As long as you didn't mess with her, she didn't mess with you."

"But she lived in England, not here?" Tom asked, confused.

"Like many people with magic powers, she straddled two worlds. Perhaps her castle still exists in Britain now."

"I don't think so," Tom said, wondering if it could be buried under something, or was tangled in a wood, or had been dismantled over the years.

Long grasses and scrubby bushes ran right up to the castle walls, where the stones were packed in tight, offering no chink of an entrance. Every now and again they caught a glimpse of towers screened by trees, and then the view would be obscured again. Brenna found she couldn't fly over the castle grounds, blocked by whatever sealed the entrance.

By the time they had made their way back to the archway, a fine drizzle had started to fall and the grey light of the afternoon was darkening to twilight. Orlas was debating with Rek whether to camp outside the walls when Nerian shouted, "Yes!"

They turned in alarm to see a white light rolling up from the ground to encompass the archway. The light then flashed away and across the walls, rippling around the entire castle. In seconds it was over and the archway stood in front of them, clear of debris. Beyond was a short tunnel through which they caught a glimpse of a courtyard.

Nerian didn't hesitate. He hurried up the tunnel and into the courtyard, where there was an unexpected sight – the castle blazed before them, every window glowing with candlelight.

Tom felt a prickle run up his spine. The spell that had sealed the entrance had also preserved it in time. The castle was not the ruin they had been expecting. He expected to see Ceridwen step out to greet them.

The courtyard was surrounded by stables, tack rooms, and other long low buildings. Ahead, the main doorway stood open, light falling on the stone steps, beckoning them forward.

"Is this real?" Beansprout asked.

"Of course, although enhanced with an enchantment I suspect," Nerian answered.

"Did you know this would happen?" Orlas asked.

"Of course not. Herne reveals little or nothing."

"So where's the cauldron?" Orlas asked, still fixated on the castle.

"He did tell me that. It's in a courtyard, somewhere in the middle of that." Nerian gestured to the castle ahead. "Shall we?"

But they all seemed strangely reluctant to cross the courtyard.

"It feels like a trap," Woodsmoke said suspiciously.

Rek grunted his agreement. "I don't trust magic after the last time."

"Magic is a tool, nothing else," Nerian told him, scathingly. "Besides, Herne would not send us to our deaths."

"Trying to convince yourself, are you?" Rek retorted. "Because you don't sound that sure!"

"Well, we're here now," Orlas said. He turned to the Cervini waiting in the shadows behind him. "Bring Merlin in to the courtyard and secure the entrance."

Arthur pulled Excalibur free of its scabbard, and glanced up at the rain laden clouds. "Let's check the main hall before we all get soaked."

Woodsmoke nodded. "You go ahead. I'll stable the horses."

"I think I'd rather camp outside," Beansprout muttered to Tom. But Arthur was already crossing to the light-filled entrance and they hurried after him.

Crossing the threshold, they found themselves in a huge reception hall filled with a soft yellow glow from the hundreds of candles tucked into alcoves and corners. Rich tapestries lined the walls, and plump cushions filled the chairs. In the centre of the room was a table set for a meal, the plates and dishes filled with hot steaming food. There were several doors leading off it. Many stood open, revealing glimpses of rooms and corridors beyond. Directly ahead was an enormous fireplace, filled with a roaring fire.

Arthur immediately set off on a circuit of the room, Rek echoing his movements on the other side.

"I don't like this," Rek muttered. "I agree with Woodsmoke. It's a trap. Has to be."

Orlas nodded, his hand running across surfaces and picking up cushions. "Everything is perfectly preserved. This is so odd. It's as if we're expected."

Brenna stood next to Tom and Beansprout. "Do we really want to stay in here?"

"At least it's dryer than outside," Tom said, putting his pack down on a chair.

"Better wet than dead," Brenna said with a grimace. "I'm going to take a look around." In a split second she changed form and flew across the room and up a staircase.

"Good idea," Rek agreed, standing by a door on the right of the hall. "I'm going to check out the rooms on this side."

"Wait," called Orlas, crossing the room to join him. "I'll come too."

They left, leaving Arthur to prowl round the main hall, poking into its nooks and crannies. Tom's stomach reminded him that it was time to eat, and he headed to the table and picked up a hot chicken leg. He was about to take a bite when Nerian yelled, "No!"

Tom dropped it in shock. "What's wrong?"

Nerian rushed to his side, followed by Beansprout. "Sorry, but I don't think we should eat or drink anything."

"I thought this place was safe?"

"I'd rather take precautions."

Nerian examined the food with the aid of a small stick he produced from his pocket.

"Do you think it's poisoned?" Beansprout asked.

"I think it's enchanted, like everything else here. We could end up asleep, or forgetful, or dead."

"But why would Herne send us here if it was so dangerous?"

"Because of Merlin." Clearly troubled, he said, "I felt something when Herne took over my body." He paused as he remembered the moment. "He was relieved, overjoyed even at finding him, and then grief stricken when he knew he was dead. It was like the emotion of a parent, or a sibling. It was so powerful."

Tom looked shocked. "Are you saying that Herne is related to Merlin?"

"It felt that way. That would explain why he's lifted a centuries-old spell on this place."

"It would also explain Merlin's natural magic," Beansprout said, thinking of Merlin's powers. "Particularly that he's a shapeshifter; that he could become a stag, like you. Did you know him?"

"No, I'm too young. He was gone by the time I was born. But everyone remembers him. He's like a father of the tribe."

"Arthur describes him as being like a father." She dropped her voice so Arthur wouldn't hear, "And he's behaved very rashly to find him too."

Tom laughed dryly. "And yet Nimue was desperate to keep him hidden. Strange isn't it, what some people are prepared to do for others."

Their conversation was interrupted by Woodsmoke coming in from the stables. He looked round and whistled. "It looks like we were expected. The stables are stocked with fresh hay and water too. Is that why you look so worried?"

"I think we're in over our heads, Woodsmoke," Beansprout said.

"I know that. Every single star out there has disappeared. The sky is black and the night is still. You could hear a pin drop. It's like everything is waiting for something to happen."

"Are the others all right?" Nerian asked, referring to the Cervini.

"They're fine, for now."

"By Herne's breath!" Nerian said, "I don't know whether it's safer for them to stay out or come in."

Woodsmoke looked around, thinking. "Bring them in, with Merlin of course. Better we should stick together, especially if a storm's coming. Shall I call them?"

Nerian nodded and Woodsmoke headed back out.

Beansprout looked pale. "I have a horrible feeling in the pit of my stomach, just like when you disappeared, Tom. Is the Cauldron the only reason this place was sealed?" she asked Nerian.

"Ceridwen was an enchantress whose Cauldron had the power of rebirth, inspiration and knowledge. Isn't that enough? Many would kill for just one of those things."

Arthur had completed his examination of the main hall, and stood by an open doorway to the left of the room. "Do you want to join me, Tom? If Rek's checking that side, we should check this one."

"Yes, I'm coming." Tom hurried across the room, his sword drawn too, leaving Nerian and Beansprout deep in conversation.

Beyond the door was a shadowy corridor. Immediately the sound of voices from the hall disappeared, and they stood in the silence waiting to see if anything moved in the shadows.

"This is too weird," Tom whispered.

Arthur turned, the pale light glinting in his eyes. "I think anything might happen tonight, Tom."

His words hung between them, and then he pressed on, Tom hard on his heels. They entered room after room, every single one lit with candles, a fire burning in the grate. And all was silent; waiting and watching.

Chapter 17 Ceridwen's Cauldron

Tom and Arthur returned to the main hall and found everyone there. Merlin's body was laid in the corner of the room on a stretcher, still wrapped in fine-scented linens designed to preserve him until the ritual.

"I suppose you found nothing either?" Rek asked, lounging in a chair in front of the fire.

"No." Arthur turned to Brenna. "You?"

"Nothing and no one." She smiled, but it didn't quite reach her eyes. "It's all too easy."

"Nevertheless, it's what we're here for. Now you're back," Orlas said, "we may as well get on with it. Any objections?"

They all shook their heads.

"I'd rather do this thing and get out of here," Rek said, rising.

Orlas turned to the other Cervini. "You two, stay here and secure the door. And you," he said, indicating the other four, "bring Merlin."

He turned to Nerian. "Lead on."

Nerian led them along the ground floor corridors towards the centre of the castle.

"Are you sure you know where you're going, Nerian?" Rek asked. "We've been this way and found nothing."

They were walking down a long corridor, whole areas of which were in virtual darkness. Nerian paused next to a section of wood-panelled wall. "Patience, Rek." He quickly explored the panel with his fingers, then said, "Found it."

With a sigh the panel slid back, revealing a dark tunnel sloping downwards. Groping inside, Nerian found a lantern hooked on the wall. Lighting it, he set off.

For Tom, the light from Nerian's lantern seemed a long way ahead; a small bobbing glow showing glimpses of stone walls and a low roof. The tunnel led downwards for a short way and then levelled off, running mostly straight. They stumbled along behind until Nerian came to a sudden stop when the tunnel split into two. He hesitated briefly and then turned right. After only a short distance they came to a flight of steps leading steeply upwards. They followed them up and round several sharp bends, the Cervini behind struggling with Merlin's body, until Nerian stopped again.

For a few seconds nothing happened, and Tom had a horrible feeling they would be stuck in the tunnels forever. Beansprout jostled against him in the dark and he could hear her shallow breaths. Then he heard a grating sound, and fresh air flooded the passage.

They tumbled out one after another into an open air courtyard. The walls were high, and in the centre of the octagonal space was a large round pool filled with water. Pale blue lights eddied lazily beneath its surface, colouring the surroundings with an unearthly pallor. They provided the only light; the courtyard was otherwise in darkness.

For a second their shuffling stilled as they gazed at the pool.

"So that's the cauldron?" Orlas asked.

Nerian nodded and crouched next to it, peering into its depths.

As Tom looked at it more closely, he saw the metal curve of the pool edge glinting in the light.

"So what now?" Rek asked, as the Cervini carrying Merlin placed him at the edge of the pool. "Do we just drop him in?"

"He's not a fish," Nerian said as he extinguished his lantern. "The pool needs to be prepared, its energies activated."

"So why seal the palace if it doesn't work?" Tom asked.

"Because many here have magic, Tom, and therefore many are capable of activating the pool with the right knowledge. And those who lack knowledge will steal and kill and maim to get it. And then use it unscrupulously."

"OK," Tom said, finally getting why the cauldron had been sealed for years.

"I need three of you to help me."

"I will," Beansprout said immediately. "What should I do?"

"Sit opposite me; you are earth. Tom?"

"Yes?"

"Sit to my left; you are water. And Brenna," he turned to find her scanning the top of the walls.

"Yes?" she said distractedly.

He gestured to his right, "If you would be so kind as to be air."

"So you are ...?" Beansprout asked, as Brenna settled herself into position.

"Fire. We sit at the four points of the compass, and as such you will help me harness fire. I want you to touch the metal edges of the cauldron, like this," and he rested his

113

hands on the lip of the pool. "We need to warm the pool and ignite its energies, and then," he looked at the others, "two of you need to carry Merlin's body into the water."

"I'll do it." Arthur's response was immediate.

"And I will," Orlas said.

"No. I will," Rek said. "You should watch. You've risked your life once already. I presume it's safe for us to enter the pool?" he asked Nerian.

"Relatively." Ignoring Rek's unfavourable response he pulled his small drum out of his pack and cradled it in his lap.

Tom watched these preparations with interest, especially as he hadn't been part of the last summoning. The four Cervini who had carried Merlin's body had positioned themselves around the courtyard and appeared relaxed, their hands resting on their sword hilts. Orlas stood next to one of them, and Woodsmoke stood leaning against the wall next to the only entrance and the stairs beyond, his keen eyes and ears missing nothing. Rek and Arthur stood behind Merlin. Tom looked uneasily at Merlin's covered body. He found it unnerving to travel with a dead man, no matter that he was wrapped in sweet-smelling linens.

The night remained still. Tom looked up at the inky blackness, where not a spark of starlight was visible. The sky seemed very low, as if it was only just above the castle ramparts. He shuddered and wondered if it was from the cold night air, or a premonition of something to come. His gaze followed the top of the high wall around the courtyard, but nothing moved.

His train of thought was broken by a noise to his right. Nerian's head had sagged downward, his chin against his chest, but his lips moved furiously; strange unintelligible mumblings that sounded guttural and threatening. A flash of light pulsed across his chest and then down to his fingers, where it turned into a flame. For a few seconds it flickered erratically and looked as if it was going out, and then it grew stronger and steadier.

Tom edged forward to make sure his hands remained touching the cauldron, and as he did the flame ran around the cauldron's rim. Tom was so shocked he almost pulled his fingers away. He gritted his teeth and prepared for the pain of the fire, but it passed over and through his fingers harmlessly, leaving a strange warm sensation.

He looked across at the others, wondering if that was it, but they continued to grip the cauldron and Nerian continued to chant, his voice growing in strength. Although the flame had gone, Tom could feel the metal growing warmer beneath him, and deep within the pool he saw an orange glow.

The chanting stopped and Nerian looked up, and again Tom started, this time shocked to see that Nerian's eyes were white, his expression vacant. The water in front of him began to swirl and the pale blue lights glowed brighter, sparking and flashing until the pool was full of incandescent light which banished the dark from the far corners of the courtyard.

Tom started to feel the strangest sensation, as if water was running through him like he was a conduit. Looking down he saw water trickling from his fingers and into the pool. Opposite him he saw Brenna's hair begin to lift in an imperceptible breeze, while Beansprout's lap filled with flowers until they tumbled around her on to the floor.

Small waves began to form, passing across the surface until they rebounded off the side, chasing each other round and round to form a frothing mass.

The silence was shattered when Nerian shouted, "Now!"

Arthur and Rek stepped into the pool. Reaching over they picked up Merlin, and in one swift movement lifted him over the rim and dipped him in the water.

The water was now warm; Tom could see steam rising off the surface, steadily getting thicker. The swirling current lifted Merlin and the linens peeled away from his body, revealing his pale face, his long white hair and beard, and the grey cloak eddying around him. Rek and Arthur no longer needed to support his body and he floated free of their grip. In unspoken agreement they swiftly left the pool and crouched dripping at the edge.

For a few seconds Merlin drifted with the current, and then he was swiftly pulled under. His body lay unmoving at the bottom of the pool, the blue lights sparking around him, nudging and prodding as if trying to wake him. The intensity of the light increased until it was almost blinding, and Merlin rose from the depths in an explosion of water, his arms flailing as he gasped for breath.

"Merlin!" Arthur cried as Tom jerked backwards in shock.

Merlin's eyes opened for the first time, his eyes as blue as the light that surrounded him. But they were wild and frightened, and he looked around at the gathered faces and uttered a string of unintelligible words. He stared beyond Arthur, looking up towards the top of the wall, and Tom heard someone laugh.

They all whirled around, but Tom knew who it was before he saw her. Nimue. She stood on the high stone wall, almost invisible against the night sky, laughing at the scene below her. *How had she found them?*

Before anyone could do anything, Merlin struggled upright and shouted again, his voice hoarse and rasping. It sounded as if he was calling someone, or something.

They all retreated now from the edges of the pool, scuttling back like crabs. Only Arthur remained close. Ignoring Nimue, he called, "Merlin, it's me, Arthur." Desperation was etched across his face.

Then several things happened at once.

Nimue raised her arm, pointing down to them as if she was about to cast a spell. Woodsmoke swiftly raised his bow and released an arrow, which thudded into her outstretched arm, and Nimue screamed and turned, outraged, towards him.

Thunder rumbled loudly from above. Deep and resonant, it echoed through the castle and out across the moors. Lightning flashed down, jagged and hot, into the courtyard, bringing shooting white lights and a whirr of wings. Statuesque figures landed around the pool and turned their backs to Merlin; bright silver daggers flashed in their hands, and they lowered long sharp spears to form a protective wall around him.

Immediately Tom and the others were on their feet, weapons drawn, but before a word was spoken, the winged creatures hauled Merlin into the air and through a rent in the cloud. Brenna streaked after them.

Thunder reverberated over the castle and lightning sizzled down again and again, forcing them to retreat against the walls for cover. One last searing lightning blast shattered the pool in an explosion of splintering metal. The water evaporated instantly, leaving a shining blue mist for a few seconds before it vanished completely, leaving them in near total darkness. One of the Cervini lit a torch, and the flare from the orange flames lit up the shocked group.

Orlas shouted to Nerian, "Nimue!"

In the shock of the attack Tom had almost forgotten her, and his head whipped around, seeking her out in the darkness. She was unconscious and lay awkwardly, her breathing shallow, blood pouring from her arm where the shattered haft of the arrow still protruded. Nerian pulled a small female doll from his pocket, an exact replica of the one he had before, and started to utter the binding spell, while Arthur slid Excalibur against her pale white throat.

He didn't move until Nerian called, "It is done."

Chapter 18 Vivian's Second Request

Sharp metal shards filled the courtyard, which was pockmarked and blackened from lightning blasts. The top of one of the walls had been blasted clean away, rubble strewn at its base, and one of the Cervini had scorch marks down the side of his body and singed eyebrows from the intense heat.

"I don't think they were trying to kill us," Orlas said, after checking no one was seriously hurt. "I think they were just trying to frighten us. And protect Merlin."

Rek struggled to his feet, dusting off bits of rubble and debris. "Well they achieved that."

"Who were they?" asked Beansprout, rubbing a trickle of blood off her arm.

Woodsmoke was looking into the night sky, his bow ready to shoot. "Sylphs – Spirits of Air."

"But why were they here?" Tom asked. "How did they know to come?"

Nerian turned from where he was examining Nimue. "Merlin summoned them, didn't you hear?"

"He did?" Tom asked, baffled. "Why?"

"He was terrified," Arthur said, his tone full of regret. "He didn't know where he was, or who we were. Not even me. Although I think he recognised Nimue." He sat on the floor at Nimue's side, reluctant to leave her even though her powers were bound.

Tom looked at the ruined pool. "And look what they've done. Did they control the storm?"

"They manipulated it, especially the lightning," Nerian explained.

"Did you understand what Merlin was saying, Arthur?" Beansprout asked.

"Some of it. He was calling them to take him home."

"Home as in England?"

"Home as in his House of Smoke and Glass."

"His what?" Tom asked, confused. "What sort of a name is that?"

"I have never been there," Arthur told them, "but he talked of it, every now and again. I never knew where it was, either, other than his 'other home' as he called it."

"It must be in the Realm of Air, then?" Tom suggested.

Rek, like Woodsmoke, was scanning the sky above them, his sword poised. "I guess it must, or why would he call the Spirits of Air?"

"Well," Orlas said wearily, "I'm disappointed he's gone so soon."

"But at least he's alive," Nerian said. "And we have Nimue."

"But no Brenna," Beansprout reminded them.

"She'll be fine," Woodsmoke said, but it sounded like he was trying to convince himself more than anybody else.

Before anyone could respond, another rumble of thunder rattled the castle and heavy rain started to fall, and they fled the courtyard.

They made their way back to the main hall, the Cervini this time carrying Nimue on the stretcher. But when they emerged from the hidden passageway they found the castle in darkness.

"What's happened?" Tom asked.

"The destruction of the cauldron has broken the spell that gave life to the castle," Nerian answered.

"So no lights, no fire, no food?"

"Exactly."

On entering the hall, Nerian headed for the fireplace while Tom lit all the candles he could find. Now the glamour of the spell had gone they could see dust lying thick along the floor and the surfaces, and the detritus of rotten food lying mouldy on the table. There was a strong smell of damp, but the building was still surprisingly intact, the floor and walls secure.

The only person who still seemed charmed by it was Arthur. "Who owns this, Orlas?"

"No one. Or me, I suppose. It lies on our land. Why?"

"I was thinking that I need a home, and this one's going spare. Would you like a tenant?" He smiled at Orlas hopefully.

Orlas laughed. "I can think of worse tenants. It's yours if you want it." He looked round, wrinkling his nose with distaste. "I certainly don't."

"Then we'll talk terms later," Arthur said, shaking hands with Orlas to secure the deal.

A small bang disturbed them and the fire roared into life under Nerian's skills, just as Brenna swooped into the hall. She collapsed on her knees in front of the flames. Water streamed from her, and she shook with cold. A slight smell of burnt feathers wafted around her.

Woodsmoke and Beansprout rushed to her side, and Woodsmoke untied his cloak and threw it around her as Beansprout said, "Are you all right?"

"I will be," Brenna answered, throwing her a small smile as she eased closer to the fire, drawing the cloak around her. "I was nearly incinerated several times. I do not recommend flying through a storm."

Arthur frowned. "But did you see where they went?"

"They headed to the Sky Meadows, as I expected, but they were too fast for me and I lost them over Dragon Skin Mountain. There was no way I could catch them. However, there really is only one place they'll be, and that's their city."

Arthur sank to the floor next to her. "Damn it."

Tom gazed around at their deflated group. All that hard work and Merlin had gone. Everyone either sat on the floor or on dusty chairs, their expressions vacant, and Tom felt their loss just as keenly. Just as he was debating what they might do next, movement in the corner of the room grabbed his attention, and a shadowy apparition slowly manifested. Tom shouted and pointed, "Something's happening!"

Rek responded quickly, rising to his feet and drawing his sword as they watched shapes swirling within its heart. Edges defined and features sharpened, and eventually Vivian appeared looking regal and imperious, her hair bound in an elaborate style, wearing a blood red gown that draped softly to the floor. She looked very different to when Tom had seen her before.

Rek advanced towards her, but Arthur stopped him, running to his side, arm outstretched. "No, Rek wait; she's not really here." He stood in front of her, as if they were really in the same room. "Vivian. We've been wondering where you've been."

"As I have you, Arthur. You've been tricky to find." She looked annoyed.

"I've been busy," he said impatiently.

"And to find you here …" Her voice trailed off as she looked around the room and saw Nimue lying motionless, guarded by two Cervini. She looked startled, and turned to Arthur accusingly. "What have you done to Nimue?"

"Nothing. She was attacked by sylphs. You should be asking what she has done to us."

Vivian ignored him and appeared to glide rather than walk across the room. She knelt at Nimue's side. Although she couldn't touch her, she examined her ashen face and injured arm, and then whirled round to face them. "That injury on her arm was not caused by a sylph."

Woodsmoke stepped forward, his voice icy. "No. It was caused by me. And if she attempts to curse any one of us again, my arrow will go straight through her heart."

Arthur intervened. "Vivian, you have no idea what Nimue has done. I suggest you listen."

"Go on," she said, crossing her arms and transferring her glare from Woodsmoke to Arthur.

"Nimue is responsible for Merlin's disappearance. She imprisoned him in a spell, and when she thought that spell might be broken and her part in it revealed, she went to investigate."

Vivian's already pallid face paled even further at this, and the accusing glare slipped from her face to be replaced by anguish.

Arthur looked confused. "You don't seem surprised, Vivian."

"I suspected, all those years ago, but I didn't know. And–" she stilled Arthur before he could interrupt, "I did not know of this when I asked you to help."

"She nearly killed Tom, Orlas and me by imprisoning us in the same spell as Merlin."

"You found him?"

"You'd better get comfortable, it's a long story."

At Vivian's request, Nerian had reluctantly cleaned Nimue's arm and manufactured a small bandage out of strips of material to wrap round it. An examination of her other injuries suggested a broken arm and a head injury. But that was all he agreed to do. Her fate, good or ill, meant little to him.

Some of the group had curled up in the shadows and gone to sleep; faint snores came from Rek. Still awake were two Cervini guarding Nimue in a far corner of the room, Tom, who lay close to the fire, and Arthur and Vivian, who sat nearby talking quietly. Tom pretended to be asleep, but was eavesdropping, peeping at them between half-closed eyes.

Vivian was arguing with Arthur. "I accept that you won't return Nimue to Avalon. I accept that you want to find Merlin. But I can't help Nimue from here, and it's clear the Cervini won't. Will you at least take her to Dragon's Hollow? It's along your route – halfway up Dragon Skin Mountain."

"That sounds a long way to go with an unwelcome guest."

"Nerian's binding spell means she can do you no harm."

"And what do I do with her in Dragon's Hollow?"

"Take her to Raghnall, that's where she was going anyway. Healing is one of his many skills. And then," she paused, thinking, "he will ensure her return to Avalon. If that's what she wants."

"And her punishment for all of this?" Arthur gestured at the room. "Do I have to remind you of what she tried to do to us?"

"I will deal with it."

"No you won't. Don't lie." Arthur looked furious.

"Merlin was my friend too."

"You used him for your own ends, Vivian, the same as you do me. You sent me to fight Morgan without telling me who she was!"

She had the grace to look sheepish. "Must I apologise again? I have already explained that I feared you wouldn't go if you knew. It's old news!"

"At least Merlin was honest in his wishes."

She laughed, a short sharp bark. "Ha! Really? He wanted you to succeed so badly he promised away your death."

"Because you made him."

"He didn't have to agree."

"You left him with little choice. He was trying to unite Britain."

"He was cementing his power," Vivian said cynically.

Arthur fell silent, his gaze falling to Excalibur sheathed at his side. The only thing Tom could hear was the crackle of the fire and the soft thump of the burning wood as it collapsed on itself.

Eventually Arthur spoke. "Being a pawn is not something I enjoy, Vivian. I will deliver Nimue to this sorcerer. And then I will find Merlin and satisfy myself he is well and safe. And then I will leave him in his tower and I will leave you on Avalon. And you will not call on me again."

Vivian narrowed her eyes questioningly.

"I mean it," he said. "I will do nothing else for you. This is my life and I will live it as I choose. Find someone else to fight your battles."

"It's thanks to me you sit here arguing."

"To deal with something you couldn't. I owe you nothing. So while I'm still feeling generous, you'd better tell me where I'm taking Nimue."

After this, Tom's tiredness overwhelmed him and he fell asleep.

They woke at dawn to find Vivian gone. Arthur had a purpose about him that Tom hadn't noticed the night before.

He announced his plans over breakfast. "I don't expect anyone to come with me, I'm going because I want to satisfy myself that Merlin's safe." He shrugged. "And then, as long as he is well, I'll leave him and return here, if I may, Orlas?"

"Of course. I will send a group from the Great Hall to make it habitable. But–" Orlas looked worried, "we can't come with you. I have duties I must attend to."

"Don't worry, Orlas," Woodsmoke said, "Arthur will have back-up."

Arthur glanced at Woodsmoke. "I said I'm happy to go alone."

"The dragon mountain is dangerous. I'll come with you."

"So will I," added Brenna.

Tom and Beansprout looked at each other in horror at the prospect of being left behind, and Beansprout said, "Obviously we're coming too."

126

Nerian looked as serious as Orlas. "Good. In that case you should take the poppet with you," he said, referring to the doll he'd used the binding spell on. "I have bound her powers again, but it's a simpler binding this time, one that does not require a spell to release it. Keep it safe, and well out of reach of Nimue. Do not underestimate the witch. Her powers may be bound, but she is not to be trusted."

Chapter 19 Around the Campfire

At last they came to the edge of the Blind Moor. It was well named. Mist rolled across its surface and pooled in hollows, obscuring the thick tufted grasses that lay underfoot. The bronze tones of sedge appeared unexpectedly, glinting in the occasional ray of weak sunshine. They proceeded slowly so the horses wouldn't stumble into hidden holes and shallow streams. At unexpected moments the mist rose, swelling and thickening until only vague images were visible.

Enisled lay behind them, lost from view. There they had said their goodbyes to the Cervini, planning to see them again on their return.

Tom sat at the back of the line, which he'd decided was his favourite place. He could see what was happening ahead and have a good look around him as they travelled. He liked that he didn't have to set the pace, and as he had no idea where they were going anyway, he was able to sit and think.

He was sick of the cold damp air and the keening wind that sliced through its muffled silence, but he liked the remote wilderness they were travelling through. They no longer saw Cervini in the distance, or even the ordinary wild deer that roamed the lowlands. Every now and again hares, their ears raised and attentive, appeared on the horizon before melting back into the land like ghosts. And once they saw a large round mound covered with smooth green grass rearing up to their left. Tom had an overwhelming urge to race over and demand entry to the Under-Palace of the old royal tribes. It reminded him of Finnlugh, and he wondered what he was doing.

Ahead he could see Arthur, and he caught a glimpse of Nimue propped in front of him on his horse. She had regained consciousness, but remained drowsy. For long periods she slept, leaning back against Arthur where he could ensure her compliance. Beansprout rode at Arthur's side, wary of Nimue's every move.

Brenna and Woodsmoke led them, picking their way down paths that snaked alongside ice cold streams. Nymphs lived in these shallow inland waters, and Tom and Beansprout craned round on their horses to see them better. They were teasing and alluring, their slender forms shining in the light and their hair cascading in green ribbons down their backs. They mostly kept to themselves, giggling to each other in little groups, watching them pass with half-hearted interest. But one, overcome with curiosity, popped up suddenly from a stream at Tom's side. She was draped in silky clothes that barely covered her, and she gazed up at him with big round eyes, casting her gaze over him appreciatively, beckoning him with a smile. Tom was so shocked he nearly fell off his horse. It was only with the greatest concentration that he kept going in the right direction.

Nightfall brought them to the base of Dragon Skin Mountain. It was low, as mountains go, and long, as if it had been stretched out. In the middle were twin peaks looking like hunched shoulders, and between these was the pass through to the Sky Meadows.

They set up camp for the night with the ease of a well-oiled machine. They had fallen into a routine in which Tom and Beansprout raised the tent and collected wood for the fire, while Woodsmoke and Brenna hunted for food – if they hadn't already caught it during the day. Arthur watched Nimue and tended the horses; Nimue watched them silently, or pretended to sleep.

After finishing a bowl of hot rabbit stew, Tom asked, "So who is it we're going to visit in Dragon's Hollow?"

"I wouldn't really call it a visit," Arthur said. "It's not a social call."

"You know what I mean," Tom said, helping himself to more food.

"Raghnall, the dragon sorcerer."

A disdainful voice added, "My jailor."

They looked to where Nimue sat, barely visible on the edges of the firelight.

"He is not your jailor, he's your healer," Arthur told her.

"I am healed," she retorted.

"No, you are not," Arthur bit back. "Your arm is broken, your shoulder is hunched, and you are still woozy from your head injury. And you were going to visit him anyway!"

"I could have made my own way."

Arthur's eyes were hard and pitiless. "Don't be ridiculous, you have been unconscious for most of the past few days. If you hadn't appeared at Ceridwen's you wouldn't be injured and we wouldn't be stuck with you."

Nimue remained silent, her face in shadow.

"Seeing as you're awake for the first time in days, tell me, how did you know where we were?" Arthur asked.

Nimue hesitated, as if wondering how much to say, then shrugged. "Oh, what does it matter? When I left the spell I travelled only as far as the top of Scar Face Fell, right above the cave. I wanted to see what happened. I felt the spell break and I heard the Cervinis' plans. So I decided to go there too."

"And would you like to explain why you imprisoned Merlin all those years ago?"

"Not really," she said, looking up and holding Arthur's gaze. "You wouldn't understand anyway."

"We were friends once; why don't you try?"

"Because being endlessly pursued by an obsessed man is something you have never experienced, and therefore you have no idea how awful it was. Everywhere I went, he was there, like a malevolent shadow. I felt suffocated." Her small frame shuddered with the memory.

Arthur looked down, momentarily awkward, while the others watched, intrigued. "I know he became a little infatuated with you."

"A little?" Nimue laughed.

"All right, a lot. I did at one point suggest he should leave you alone."

"You did?" Her voice softened a little.

"Yes, but he denied it and said I was imagining things."

They again fell silent, looking at each other across the fire, and it seemed to those watching that the years had disappeared, and so had they, and that Nimue and Arthur were sitting alone around the fire.

"I'd had enough, so I used his own spell against him. And I was glad I did," she added, her eyes flashing again with malice. "I got my life back."

"So why go back to the cave?"

"Because when I heard the rock fall had revealed the caves, I feared that the spell had been broken and he would come after me, for revenge. Or that his obsession would start over again. The thought filled me with dread."

Arthur sighed. "I can understand that, but why trap us in the spell too?"

"You saw what was happening. The spell had held, but Orlas insisted on me releasing it, and then he would have dragged me back to that cell. I saw a way out and I took it. Trapping you in that spell was the only way I could get out. It wasn't personal."

"So you would have come and released us, eventually?" The question was laced with disbelief.

She squirmed. "I don't know. But I'm glad you are out. My fight is not with you, Arthur, it never has been. If it helps, I promise that I won't harm you or your friends."

"I hope you mean that, Nimue. Because getting out of that spell took the intervention of Herne, and it nearly killed us."

"I'm sorry. And sorry to you too, Tom." For the first time since waking she looked at him and smiled. He had no idea what to say, so he just stared at her, stupidly. She didn't seem to notice, instead saying, "I used to help you, Arthur. We made a good team. All those people coming and going from Camelot. I miss it." She hesitated before adding crossly, "I told you not to go chasing after that fool Lancelot. That's when it all went wrong. She wasn't worth it."

Tom knew why she'd hesitated and he looked at Arthur, wondering how he'd react, but he was calm.

"Please don't talk about Guinevere that way. I had to go. And the rest is history."

Nimue was now animated, her hostility gone, and she seemed keen to re-establish her old friendship with Arthur. "You won't know this, obviously, but I was one of the nine priestesses who carried you to Avalon. That was a sad day,

Arthur. Very sad. I cried for a week. I only crossed back to Britain a few times after that."

"Why? What happened?" He leaned forward, eager to hear her response.

"It was as if the whole world had gone mad. It was chaotic, frightening; full of warmongering men and invading tribes. I hated it. And there was nothing I could do. Nothing." She sounded bitter and angry. "So I came here to live, as did some of the other priestesses. The old ways were failing there, but not here."

"That sounds similar to something Morgan said. So why didn't you stop her when she started killing the Aerikeen – Brenna's kin?" He indicated to where Brenna sat.

Nimue glanced at Brenna and her face changed as if suddenly realising who she was. "Sorry, that was slow of me. Of course you are Aerikeen. Morgan was half-fey and far stronger than me, than any of us, except the fey. So Vivian thought of you Arthur. You scared Morgan."

"Ha! She'd outgrown her fear of me. If it hadn't been for Finnlugh we'd all be dead."

"Well, she is gone and you are here. And it is so good to see you." She flashed her brilliant smile again.

"I'd like to believe you, Nimue, but I'm not sure I can," Arthur said softly.

Silence fell and Nimue's smile faltered, and Tom realised they were all wondering how far they could trust Nimue.

Eventually Brenna spoke, changing the subject. "I hear Raghnall is a great man. He subdued the dragons and won the pass for the fey, allowing access to the Sky Meadows."

"And allowed himself access to the ancient dragon caves riddling the mountain," Nimue retorted.

"You disapprove of him then?" Brenna asked.

"I disapprove of him proclaiming to be a great man while all along he grubs for the bright gems of the dragons and makes deals with the sylphs."

"I suppose he felt he deserved some reward for his efforts."

"He certainly has that. He lives in splendour; they all do up there. Have you ever been to Dragon's Hollow?"

"Never."

She turned to Woodsmoke. "Have you?"

He shook his head. "No."

"Well, you'll soon see," Nimue said. "The place is dripping in gold and gems."

"Why are you going to see him?" Woodsmoke asked.

"Dragon's Hollow is the best source of gems and metals; there are some we need for spells which we cannot get from anywhere else. And we have known him a long time." Nimue didn't elaborate.

Tom had been following this conversation with interest, and he finally burst out, "Do you mean there are dragons on the mountain?"

"Yes," Brenna answered, "but they have been driven to the outer reaches, the far passes and the deepest caves. I have heard that the main path up the mountain is generally clear."

Tom's mouth fell open. Recovering quickly, he turned to Arthur. "Did you know?"

"Vivian warned me," he said, nodding.

And as if to validate their discussion, a long, low, rumbling roar rolled down the mountain. Tom felt his skin prickle and a shiver ran down his spine.

"Don't worry," Arthur said, "I killed a few back in my other life."

"In England?" Beansprout asked excitedly.

"In Britain," Arthur corrected.

Tom frowned. "But I thought that was a myth."

"And you used to think magic didn't exist, either," Arthur said, a trace of a smile on his lips.

"So will the dragons fly down here, off the mountain?"

Woodsmoke answered. "They are bound to the mountain; part of the great spell. Before that the land was burnt and the mountain was impassable. The path to the north led far round the mountain, and the Sky Meadows were inaccessible for all except those who could fly, and the air spirits themselves."

"And the Sky Meadows are ...?"

"The way to the Realm of Air. Where we find Merlin."

Chapter 20 The Attractions of Magic

The trail they followed the next day was well used and followed a gentle gradient, winding up through the folds of the mountain as it slowly climbed higher and higher. They travelled through low brush and shrubs and then through stands of trees, some ancient, some only a few years old, new growth following fires. And every now and again they saw the bleached white bones of dragons shining in the sunlight.

Beansprout had dropped back to speak to Tom. "What do you think of magic, Tom?"

He looked at her, puzzled. "I don't know. It's just there I suppose."

She rolled her eyes in frustration. "But aren't you fascinated by it? It exists. It's real. You tried to do some!"

"I thought I was going to die trapped in a spell forever. It was a motivating moment."

"But how did it feel?" At his blank look she elaborated. "You know, when you read the spell and assembled all the things you needed, and then started to read it. How did it feel? Did your fingers tingle? Did the air change? What happened?"

"I don't know. I had no idea what I was doing. I didn't even think it would work. In fact I don't think it did. Herne appeared and everything went Boom." He threw his hands wide to demonstrate.

"So you didn't feel anything?"

"No."

Beansprout took a deep breath. "OK. Well what did it feel like in the spell?"

This time he had no hesitation. "That was weird!"

"Weird how?"

"Everything felt so ancient, as if I was trapped in time – you know, like one of those mosquitoes trapped in amber in Jurassic Park."

"I'm not completely stupid, Tom. So it felt different?"

"Hugely different. Like time had no meaning. No–" he paused, considering. "More like I was outside time. Completely removed from it." He looked ahead to where Nimue sat with Arthur. "It was immense. And terrifying."

"Immense, that's the word," she said enthusiastically. "That's what I felt around the cauldron. Did you feel the energy then?"

He nodded, remembering. "Yes, it was like an electric current. You had flowers in your lap."

"It was the most amazing feeling. I felt connected to everything. I could feel this power surging up through me, like a spring. And I felt I was a small part of something really huge. I want to be able to do that."

Now she had Tom's full attention. "Do you?" he asked, alarmed.

"Yes. Don't you?"

"No. It's dangerous. It's too big."

"Well I'd have to learn. Properly. Nimue did, she's human and look what she can do."

"And she's dangerous," he said, as if that proved his point.

"Not really. It seems to me that Merlin was too persistent and she'd had enough. She had the ability to do something about it, so she did. Everything else was self-preservation."

Tom started to feel annoyed. "So it was OK to put me in a spell?"

"No, of course not, that's not what I'm saying. She misused her power and over-reacted. And has since apologised. But she obviously felt vulnerable."

Tom narrowed his eyes at her. "You're defending her? Because I can assure you she did not appear the slightest bit vulnerable at the time."

"She might not have appeared it, but I bet she felt it! It's a reasonable reaction under the circumstances."

"I can't believe you're taking her side!"

"Someone needs to. Didn't you listen last night? Can't you imagine what it must have felt like? To have to put up with that constant attention?"

They had stopped and were now shouting at each other, their horses fretful, sensing the tension.

"I'm sure Merlin didn't mean it."

"I'm sure he did. He didn't stop, did he? Selfish old bastard."

The others became aware of the noise and whirled round.

"Are you OK?" Arthur called.

"We're fine," they both yelled, glaring at each other.

Arthur looked relieved and then confused. "Are you sure?"

"Yes!"

"Well, keep up then," and he waved Woodsmoke and Brenna on, following them up the slope.

Beansprout's voice dropped and she hissed at Tom as they started moving again. "If it was me and I had Nimue's skills, I'd do the same thing. And I would like to think that as my friend and cousin, you would be on my side, instead of being overawed by the tales of some old man."

She spurred her horse on, leaving Tom on his own.

They halted for lunch, turning off the trail and sheltering from the sun beneath the spreading branches of a grove of old trees. Close by, a narrow stream wound through the undergrowth.

"Why is it getting hotter?" Beansprout asked as she dismounted. "Shouldn't it be colder as we get higher up the mountain? Not that I'm complaining – it's great."

Nimue answered as she slid to the ground, holding her arm awkwardly and grimacing. "This place has a different climate to what you'd expect. It was designed that way because the fey in the Hollow like it hot. The unfortunate thing is, the dragons like it too."

"Oh." Beansprout's enthusiasm was slightly dimmed. "By the way, Nimue, when we have a chance later, I'd like to ask you a few questions."

Tom stopped halfway through getting his pack off his horse and looked over at Beansprout. She caught him staring, but ignored him and turned back to Nimue. Nimue was oblivious. "Of course, whatever I can help you with. You're Beansprout, is that right? I think that's what Arthur told me."

"Yes, Tom's cousin. I'm so glad he's here," she said, smiling in a sickly way at Tom. "He's so much fun to have around."

A distant roar rocked the ground beneath their feet, ending their conversation. Apart from Nimue, everyone withdrew their weapons.

"That sounded closer than I'd like," Woodsmoke said, scanning the sky.

They heard another roar, even closer.

"Is it coming for us?" Tom asked, alarmed.

"The dragons shouldn't be this close to the main path," Nimue answered, "but maybe something's attracting this one's attention."

She turned to Arthur. Excalibur gleamed in a ray of sun. "Your sword, Arthur. It hears it. That's what draws it close."

"What do you mean, it hears it?" Arthur asked.

"It is made from the precious metals of the fey by the Forger of Light; it's imbued with spells for protection and strength. It sings of where it was and where it is, as do all fey weapons of this quality."

"But what about Woodsmoke's weapons, and Brenna's? They're obviously faerie made too."

"But they were not made with spells by the Forger of Light. Excalibur is a weapon of peculiar powers, Arthur. And dragons like such weapons. The singing comforts them."

"You might have mentioned this before, Nimue," Arthur said angrily, as the others warily eyed Excalibur.

"I honestly didn't think," she snapped.

"So if it comforts them," Tom said as another roar sounded, "why does it sound so annoyed?"

"I presume because it wants Excalibur but doesn't have it yet," Woodsmoke answered, as a large shadow fell across them.

They looked up to see the scaly underside, powerful legs and broad wings of a dragon passing overhead.

"You should go. Leave me here, I can fight it alone," Arthur told them.

They watched as the dragon turned and flew back in their direction. It shimmered bright blue and green in the sunlight. As it grew closer they could see its long neck and head, and its narrow red eyes. Tom couldn't believe he was actually seeing a dragon, and from the pale look on Beansprout's face, neither could she.

"It's too late for that, Arthur," Woodsmoke said, stepping out from under the trees' cover and releasing an arrow at the dragon's vulnerable abdomen. He called back over his shoulder. "Someone protect the horses!"

Nimue and Beansprout quickly retreated into the trees beyond the stream with the horses, which were now starting to panic. Tom heard Nimue shout, "Further back Beansprout, much further! Arthur, this would be a good time to restore my powers."

Arthur shouted back, "Good try Nimue, but no thanks."

Woodsmoke continued to fire arrows with unerring accuracy, a handful sinking into the dragon's flesh, the others bouncing off its thick skin. It roared again, possibly in pain, but to Tom it sounded more like anger. It dropped onto the path in front of them, crushing the surrounding bushes, and they ran back to the trees, desperately seeking cover.

The dragon was easily as big as a house. Its long neck ended with a sharp angular head, its jaw filled with razor-sharp teeth, and its red eyes blazed. Thick scales like armour plating covered its body and neck, wrapping around its chest like a breastplate. Its broad wings flexed across its back and smoke steamed out of its long nose as it probed forward, its tail thumping and slithering along. Tom could feel the ground shaking.

For a brief second they froze as it raised its head, sniffing deeply. Arthur seized his moment and bounded out from the shadows, running with Excalibur extended before him. But the dragon immediately dropped its head and shot a long tongue of fire at Arthur, causing him to roll to his right. The dragon lunged after him.

Brenna, Woodsmoke and Tom rushed forward to distract it. With swords drawn, they rushed beneath its outspread wings and jabbed at any soft fleshy parts they could see.

The dragon roared and flames shot out, burning the dry grasses and shrubs in a wide semi-circle. Its huge muscular tail thrashed, and Tom rolled and scrambled out of the way, hacking awkwardly with his sword. One of the dragon's wings clipped Woodsmoke, sending him reeling backwards.

Tom weaved beneath the bulk of the dragon, avoiding its stamping feet as it trampled the baked earth. Uselessly he stabbed upwards at the dragon's soft underbelly, but he could barely reach it, and his sword only pricked its skin. He watched as the others ran to and fro, dodging around its flapping wings and streams of fire. The dragon brushed them aside like flies. Tom was so close to being squashed he couldn't keep track of what was happening, then just as he was planning to dive out from under the dragon, Arthur skidded to a halt next to him. Again Tom stabbed wildly upwards, but Arthur was far more accurate and he wielded Excalibur expertly. He drove the blade into the soft flesh and pulled the sword along its belly, the blade moving easily, as if through butter.

"Tom, move – now!" yelled Arthur, as hot blood and guts fell to the ground and the dragon's legs started to crumple.

They both dived outwards as its body hit the ground. The dragon was dying, but it continued to attack, spraying fire in all directions, grass and trees flaring into flames. But the bursts of fire became shorter and weaker as the dragon's head dropped lower and lower. Woodsmoke and Brenna hacked at its neck, their swords barely denting its thick scales.

Arthur raced across the smouldering grass and stood next to them. He raised Excalibur high above his head and then brought it down in one swift stroke. It sliced through the neck cleanly, severing the dragon's head from its body.

For a few seconds the dragon's long neck thrashed about, blood spurting from the open wound before pooling thickly on the ground, then it crashed to the floor.

Tom staggered to his feet, gasping for breath and coughing. A veil of smoke choked the air and he trampled down the flames where they licked the dry grass. His eyes stung and he blinked rapidly as he made his way over to the severed head, the dragon's eyes glazing over already.

Nimue's voice disturbed the silence. "You must cut out the heart."

She stood on the edge of the charred clearing, Beansprout next to her. They carried large bundles of bush they had been using to beat out the flames, and were singed and black with soot. Beansprout had a smear of blood across her cheek.

"Why?" Arthur leant against the dragon, breathing heavily.

"Here, in the Other, dragons have many special properties they do not have anywhere else. They live for gold, gems and precious metals, because part of them is made of those things. After death, parts of the body transform into jewels, except for the heart. It must be cut out immediately after death; only then will it transform into a gem that is highly prized here – dragonyx. And by cutting out its heart you claim the dragon as yours, which means you keep all profits from its body."

Arthur looked confused. "That's crazy."

"It's true," Woodsmoke agreed, "or at least, so I've heard."

Woodsmoke and Brenna were trying to stop the fire spreading, kicking dirt over patches of flames, and hacking off burning branches before whole trees could catch.

"I have no wish to butcher the creature any further," Arthur answered. "And besides, it's huge. It will take too long."

He was right. The dragon had brought down several trees and now completely blocked the path with its bulk. It had fallen forward onto its chest and stomach, and its enormous wings had wrapped around its front and sides as it had tried to protect itself from further attack.

"Arthur," Nimue sighed. "You have no money here, no prestige. This will give you security. And although this isn't the biggest dragon I've seen, it's big enough. And hardly anyone sees dragonyx any more."

Arthur hesitated, clearly tempted.

"As much as I hate to agree with Nimue," Woodsmoke said, "she's right."

"But the longer we stay here, the more at risk we are. We could be attacked again," Arthur reasoned.

"Then I suggest we're quick," Woodsmoke said decisively. "We'll take the heart, eat on the road, and get to Dragon's Hollow before dark. As fun as this was, I don't particularly want to be attacked again. And," he added, "it means you won't have to run errands for Vivian again." He looked pointedly at Nimue.

Ignoring Woodsmoke's jibe, Nimue walked over to Tom. "May I?" she asked, indicating his sword.

Tom handed it to her wordlessly, and they watched as Nimue pulled the wing aside with Woodsmoke's help and thrust the sword into the dragon's right chest. It barely pierced its horny skin.

"Right here," she said to Arthur.

Arthur started cutting into the dragon's side, around the spot Nimue had indicated. Hot, thick blood oozed out of the gaping wound, splashing him. He stripped off his shirt and removed his boots.

Woodsmoke pulled his hunting knife from his pack and helped Arthur slice through the layers of muscle and bone. "I'm afraid I'm not much help, Arthur. I haven't carved open many dragons."

"That's all right – I'm not planning on doing this again." Arthur hacked and carved and hacked and carved, stopping and starting until he could see what he was looking for. Thick muscles and wiry tendons glistened in the light.

"Is that gold?" Arthur asked, seeing a glint of yellow along a huge ropey tendon.

"Probably," Nimue said, trying to get a better look.

Arthur straightened up. "Is this another reason dragons are hunted?"

"You made this look easy, Arthur," Nimue said wryly. "Many perish trying to kill dragons. There are probably as many bones of fey here as bones of dragons. That's why the city needs Raghnall's spell."

"Well when I see this sorcerer," Arthur said, continuing his grizzly business, "I'll tell him his spells aren't working."

"Perhaps because Excalibur is stronger," Nimue said softly.

Chapter 21 Blood and Bone

After a long bloody battle with sinew and tendon, Arthur finally extracted the dragon's heart. He was slick with blood, and Woodsmoke wasn't much cleaner. While Woodsmoke washed his arms at the edge of the stream, Arthur stood in the middle, sluicing water over himself and scrubbing his skin with grass to get rid of the blood that had hardened in the sun.

When he was clean, Arthur turned to the heart. It sat on the bank streaked with dried blood. "I suppose I'd better clean this," he said to the others, who had crowded round. "I thought we were going to eat on the road?" he added, noticing they were munching on dried meats and cheese.

"That was before we realised slicing out a dragon's heart was going to take half the afternoon," Tom said, through a mouthful of food.

"An hour is not half the afternoon."

Arthur had worked quickly, but extracting the heart without damaging it had taken longer than expected. He'd needed Woodsmoke's advice on slicing through arteries as thick as his arms, and the enormous muscles that anchored it.

The heart was big – the size of a cartwheel – and was an irregular round shape. At the moment it was covered in gunk. It looked like an ugly chunk of flesh, and it smelt rotten, like fungus-filled earth that had never seen the sun. But as Arthur scrubbed it clean it began to transform and shine in the sun. Slowly a pale ruby red stone was revealed. The surface was mostly pitted and cloudy, but clear lucent patches began to appear, allowing them a glimpse inside the stone, where they saw thick veins of gold, and a black star in the centre.

"That's clean enough for now," Arthur said, satisfied.

"The gem workers of the Hollow will polish it up. You won't recognise it once they've finished with it," Nimue said.

Woodsmoke fetched a large blanket from his pack. "Here, use this."

They rolled the gem in the blanket and secured it to the tent poles strapped to one of the horses.

"What do I do with the rest of it?" Arthur looked at the dragon carcass. Its bright green and blue scales still shone in the sun, and from the path you couldn't see the wound in its side, or tell that its head had been separated from its neck. It looked like it was sleeping.

Nimue struggled back on to Arthur's horse. "The goblins will come and collect it soon enough."

"I can't believe I've seen a dragon! And then Arthur killed it," Beansprout said to Tom, a note of sadness in her voice, as they rode up the mountain. The two of them had spent some time examining the dragon while Arthur carved out the heart, feeling its hard skin and thick scales.

"Well yeah," Tom agreed. "But it would have killed us, so …"

Beansprout had managed to free a scale from the dragon's body, and she turned it over in her hands, admiring the way it glistened in the sun. "Look at it!" she said. "It's so beautiful. What do you think they'll do with the rest of the body?"

"Break it down like an old car, by the sound of it. From what Brenna said, there's a whole industry built around dragons and their gold. You could have that made into something. Maybe a decoration for your bow, or your knife hilt."

"I suppose so, although it seems a bit grizzly," Beansprout said, re-pocketing the scale.

Woodsmoke had picked up the pace after their stop, and as the sun dipped to the horizon they neared Dragon's Hollow. They were high on the mountain and the two peaks rose ahead of them, the path leading to the natural depression between. The road widened and flattened, and as they rounded a bend the great walls of the town came into view. The gates were made of burnished rose gold, and on them, inlaid in silver and black metal, was an ornately carved roaring dragon, its wings spread in flight. The high city walls were solidly built of thick stone, extending on both sides to the edge of the peaks. Along the top, carved stone dragons glowered menacingly.

"Is this wall to keep dragons out?" Tom asked, thinking surely that was impossible.

"No," Nimue answered. "Nothing keeps dragons out – except the sorcerer's spell. The wall is to keep out those who would attack the Hollow. And that really would be foolish, so no one has tried for a long time."

"So why such enormous gates?" Beansprout asked.

"Because it looks good, and besides, you never know. Sometimes people do stupid things for gold." Nimue shrugged.

"How do we get in?" Arthur asked.

Nimue pointed to the small figures on top of the wall. "The sentries will let us in."

As they approached, the gates began to swing slowly back, revealing a cavernous tunnel beyond. A booming trumpet call echoed out of the tunnel, and half a dozen fey on horseback came to meet them. They were richly dressed in bright silks, and their horses had elaborate bridles, their manes woven with strips of silver and gold material.

Instinctively, Woodsmoke, Arthur and Brenna reached for their weapons, but Nimue stopped them, saying in harsh whisper, "Wait!"

An imperious fey, dressed in rich scarlet, led the group. His hair was as red as his clothing, and he had a long beard plaited with silver thread. He bowed his head briefly before addressing Arthur. "Who do we have the honour of welcoming, mighty dragon slayer?"

Tom wondered how they could possibly know about the dragon, when Arthur answered smoothly and courteously. "I am Arthur, King of the ancient Britons, Boar of Cornwall, Twice Born, Wielder of Excalibur gift of the Forger of Light. To whom do I owe the pleasure of this welcome?"

"Magen, Chief Slayer of the Dragon Guard." He stared at Arthur, a hint of challenge flashing in his eyes. "We are here to escort you to Dragon's Hollow. The Sorcerer requests your presence."

"Well," said Arthur evenly, giving a smile that wasn't quite a smile, "it's fortunate that it is the sorcerer we are here to meet."

Magen raised his hand, and from out of the tunnel behind him came a huge eight-wheeled cart pulled by four large purple lizards. On the back of the cart were a number of big burly creatures covered with warts and thick green skin.

"Goblins," Woodsmoke explained to Tom.

"The dragon belongs to Arthur," Nimue said to Magen. "He has the dragonyx." She nodded to where it hung behind Woodsmoke.

If possible, Magen looked even more annoyed. "In that case, the sorcerer requests your permission to bring back the dragon body for dismemberment."

"My permission?" Arthur asked, clearly confused.

"As the dragon belongs to you and not the city, you must agree to its dismemberment. You will receive all monies as are due to you, minus the fee for transformation," Magen explained impatiently.

"In that case," Arthur said, "yes I do."

As the cart trundled past them, Magen turned. "Follow me."

The temperature dropped once they were in the tunnel, and Magen was visible only as a dark silhouette ahead until they emerged into a small square dappled in the cool purple shadows of twilight. Around it was a warren of buildings and narrow lanes. In the pale light the buildings shimmered from the dusting of gold that patterned the stone.

They continued down a long central avenue, passing beneath balconies with cascading flowers and greenery. The place looked wealthy and well cared for, the buildings ornate with detailed embellishments in metals of many colours. This was a very different place from the Meet. Occasionally they passed locals wandering back from the town centre, dressed in fine linens with trimmings of embroidery and lace.

Dragon's Hollow was well named, as it sat encircled by the shoulders of the two peaks on either side. It had trapped the heat of the day so that as night fell, warmth poured from the golden stone around them. Tom grew sticky and tired and wondered impatiently how long it would take to get to the sorcerer. He began to daydream of cold showers and icy drinks, but when they rounded the next corner, all such thoughts left his mind rapidly. They stumbled to a halt and looked around, awestruck.

In front of them was a large perfectly round lake, from which rose an enormous dragon fountain made of coloured glass, precious metals and luminous gems. Like the dragon on the gate, its wings were spread in flight, and its head was looking down upon them. Instead of flames, water poured from its mouth.

Palatial buildings were set around the pool and against the curved bowl of the peaks. In the dusk, the buildings glittered with thousands of lights. Hundreds of faeries milled about the central space, strolling around the pool and across the bridges that spanned it. Entertainers had set up in nooks, and at the start of the bridge ahead was a group of fire-breathing faeries, shooting flames of orange, blue and green high into the sky.

The first person to find their voice was Brenna. "I had no idea of the scale of this place."

"We seek to keep its splendours to ourselves." Magen stood next to them, waiting until they were ready to follow him.

"I can tell why," Arthur murmured.

"Some of the greatest weapons of faerie are made here," Magen said proudly.

"Is this where the Forger of Light lives?" Arthur asked.

"Not any more."

Changing the subject, Magen pointed to the far side of Dragon's Hollow, to a vast house on the mountainside, glittering with inlaid silver and rich black marble. Its many windows lay in darkness, except for the top of the house, where a solitary light burned. "That's where we are heading – The House of the Beloved."

Chapter 22 House of the Beloved

Magen led the way across town to the bottom of a long drive bordered with topiary. The guards remained at the gate while the others carried on up to the sorcerer's house, stopping at the bottom of a flight of steps where Arthur carefully unloaded the dragonyx. Leaving their horses with two grooms, they followed Magen into the main building.

They were obviously expected. The doors stood wide, allowing what little breeze there was to flow down the hall. Hundreds of candles flickered, reflecting off the marble floors. They followed Magen up a staircase and along a corridor, eventually coming out onto a broad covered balcony overlooking the city. A long table was set for dinner, and at the far end was a smaller table of drinks.

"Raghnall will join you soon. In the meantime, help yourself to drinks," said Magen, gesturing to the table.

"You're not staying?" Arthur asked.

"My father and I don't exactly see eye to eye," Magen replied, and left abruptly.

"His father! Interesting," Woodsmoke said, heading to the drinks table.

"I'd forgotten he had children," Nimue said. "I've never met them. It doesn't surprise me they don't get on, though."

Woodsmoke passed her a glass of wine. "Why's that?"

"Because he's a pompous ass," she hissed before taking a healthy swig of wine.

"Needed that did you, Nimue?" Brenna said with a wry smile.

"Yes, it's been quite a day. And it's going to get worse," Nimue grumbled.

They took their drinks over to the balustrade and stood looking out across the city below. Darkness had fallen and stars glittered above them, mirroring the hundreds of flickering lamps below. The night air was silky smooth across their skin.

"This place looks too good to be true," Brenna observed.

Woodsmoke nodded. "I had no idea how much dragon's gold there was here."

"I have heard tales about it, but I never envisioned it could be this ..." Brenna struggled for words.

Arthur finished her sentence. "Magnificent?"

"I knew you'd like this place," Nimue said, from where she had taken a seat in the shadows.

"It reminds me of Camelot."

Beansprout's mouth fell open with shock. "Camelot looked like this!"

"I don't think it was quite as big as the Hollow," Nimue said, amused.

"Maybe not," Arthur said testily. "But it was beautiful, especially after Merlin embellished it a little."

"I loved Camelot, but I don't love the Hollow," Nimue said.

"Why not?" asked Tom.

"There's just too much of it. It exhausts me."

"Sometimes," Woodsmoke said, "the fey like to put on a display of wealth to dazzle and impress. You saw that, Tom, in Finnlugh's Under-Palace."

Tom nodded, thinking of the ballroom and the ornate library he had seen. "It's true, everything about The House of Evernight was extravagant. Finnlugh was extravagant. The Duchess of Cloy was extravagant!"

"As King of the Britons," Arthur said, "I can assure you I was extravagant too. Camelot was a vision of silver towers, thick walls, flags, might and wealth. It was necessary. It was meant to terrify and awe everyone who saw it."

A deep voice interrupted their conversation. "I hope the richness of your surroundings isn't upsetting you?"

They turned abruptly and saw a tall man standing in the doorway to the balcony. It was difficult to see him clearly in the low lighting, and Tom wondered how long he'd been standing there listening to their conversation. He also wondered how rude they had sounded.

"Only me," Nimue called out, "but you already know that, Raghnall."

Ignoring Nimue, Arthur answered, "Not at all. It is very pleasant after being on the road for so many weeks, and we appreciate your hospitality. I am Arthur." He held out his hand.

Raghnall stepped forward to shake his hand, and the lights on the balcony flared brightly, allowing them to see him clearly for the first time. He had thick black hair, streaked with grey, lightly oiled and swept back into a long plait. Keeping it neatly in place was a thinly beaten silver band that rested on his forehead, like a crown. He had a small, neat, triangular beard, and intense dark eyes that swept across them all imperiously before briefly resting on Nimue. His regal appearance was enhanced by his clothing. He wore a three-quarter-length coat of shimmering dark blue velvet over a shirt of fine embroidered linen, and knee-length soft leather boots. Rings adorned his fingers, and as Raghnall shook their hands Tom watched them twinkle in the lamplight.

"I am pleased you like it here. Every effort is made to provide comfort and pleasure. Not many are as immune as Nimue," he said, looking at her pointedly.

"I'm not immune, just overwhelmed," she said, rising to kiss his cheek.

"Anyone would think you starved yourself of beauty on Avalon. And I know that's not true," Raghnall said.

Nimue looked impatient. "Now now, Raghnall, let's not do that again."

"Of course not."

Tom wondered what they were referring to.

"There is food prepared for you all. I presume you are hungry – after all, dragon slaying is tiring work," Raghnall said, his eyes glittering.

"And how is it you know we slayed a dragon, Raghnall?" Arthur leaned back against the balustrade as if he owned the place.

"The lookouts along the wall." Raghnall walked over to the table and poured himself a small drink of something black and viscous. "Vivian had informed me of your impending arrival, so we were keeping an especially close watch." He turned to Nimue, smiling indulgently. "And naturally I am more than happy to help you recover, Nimue. You will of course stay here. I have prepared a room for you – for all of you, actually," he said, his gaze sweeping across them.

"We couldn't impose," Woodsmoke said. "Just direct us to the nearest inn."

"No! It's far too late. I insist." His hand flew up, palm outwards, as if to stop further discussion. "And besides, I have a large house as you can see."

For some reason, despite their opulent surroundings, Tom wasn't entirely sure he wanted to stay at the House of the Beloved, and he sensed the others felt the same – Woodsmoke's protestations weren't just from politeness. Ever since they had entered Raghnall's house, Tom had felt uncomfortable, and the fact that Vivian seemed to be an old friend didn't reassure him. Maybe he was picking up on Nimue's mood. And he was tired and sweaty and wanted a bath and clean clothes.

As if reading Tom's thoughts, Raghnall said, "But I am so thoughtless. You must want to wash and change."

As he finished speaking a bell rang throughout the house, and in seconds a small dark-haired faery materialised in the doorway. He bowed deeply. "My lord?"

"Please escort our guests to their rooms." Raghnall nodded to them. "Dinner will be in an hour. Nimue, I will come and see to your injuries." He then strolled to the edge of the balcony and gazed across the vista below, and with that they were dismissed.

Tom had never stayed in a five-star hotel, but imagined this would be a very similar experience. His room was enormous, and it contained the biggest bed he had ever seen, covered in sheets of silk and linen, and the most enormous puffy pillows. The furnishings were as bright as the marble was dark. Thick rugs covered the floor and paintings hung from the walls. A door led to an ensuite bathroom where the bath was filled with hot steaming water smelling of cedar. Thick towels hung on a stand to the side. His bags were in his room, unpacked, and his clothes were clean and fresh. Tom doubted even a five-star hotel could do that so quickly.

Tom soaked in the tub wishing he could stay there for hours. Whatever was in the water was soothing his aching muscles, and he scrubbed himself clean with an energy he hadn't felt in days.

Feeling refreshed, Tom met the others in the hall outside his room. "How long are we staying here?" he asked.

"Considering our long days on the road and the journey ahead, I think we should stay a few nights," Arthur said. "If Raghnall has no objections."

"I agree," Brenna said. "We could use the rest. You can put up with us for a few more days, Nimue?"

Nimue looked better than she had done in days. Her eyes were bright, and she was no longer hunched over from her injured shoulder. "It's fine with me – anything to put off being alone here with Raghnall."

Arthur rolled his eyes. "I doubt you'll be alone, Nimue. Besides, he's not that bad."

"You wait. You haven't spent an evening with him yet. Anyway, the longer you're here, the better I get. I may be able to come with you!"

"I think you jest, Nimue. I doubt you wish to see Merlin so soon, especially with the sylphs. And he certainly won't want to see you."

She smirked. "You may be right. But will you at least release my binding?"

"Only once we've left."

"Why not now?" Nimue glared at Arthur.

"Because I said so," he said, sounding like he was talking to a child.

"Perhaps," intervened Woodsmoke, "we should discuss this later. I'm starving." And with that he led the way downstairs, the others quickly following.

Dinner was elaborate, delicious and uncomfortable. As good as the food tasted, Tom couldn't wait for it to be over. Nimue was right. Raghnall was an insufferable show-off, a tedious bore. The conversation flowed, but only because Arthur, Beansprout and Brenna worked hard to be sociable; the rest of them struggled.

The longer the evening went on, and the more Raghnall showed off, the more competitive Arthur became. And unfortunately for Raghnall, when Arthur put his mind to it, he was very good at storytelling. Arthur didn't usually boast, so Tom could tell Raghnall was annoying him. The sorcerer relayed a long tale about a large party he had thrown for the visiting sylphs. He described the food, the decorations, the lights, the clothes, and then the music. Tom stifled a yawn.

And then Arthur started. "The week of my coronation was idyllic! Merlin surpassed himself. I have never seen Camelot look more beautiful, its towers more gilded, or the decorations so sumptuous. The visiting princes and their wives were a vision, and the feasting and hunting were unmatched in their success."

Tom caught Raghnall's expression across the table and quickly glanced away for fear he should laugh. He decided to concentrate on his food. Woodsmoke was watchful and monosyllabic, and Nimue was amused.

Raghnall asked them about their travels, but already seemed to know exactly what they had been up to. "So Nimue, Vivian tells me you had a problem with Merlin?"

"Yes, Raghnall, I did. What of it?" she challenged.

"Being trapped in a spell for centuries seems a harsh punishment," he said, "for love."

"Oh! That's what you call it? Strange, it didn't feel like that to me," she said, artfully spearing a piece of beef.

"But a highly impressive spell, nevertheless." He raised his glass to her before taking a sip.

"Not so impressive when you're trapped in it," Arthur said with a sidelong glance at Nimue.

Nimue dropped her head and looked at the table.

"Vivian gave me little information," said Raghnall, "so–"

"No surprise there," Arthur interrupted.

"I'm curious. How did you get out of it?" Raghnall continued, ignoring Arthur's tone.

"Tom prepared the ingredients to break the spell, and Herne finished it off," Arthur said airily, as if it had been the easiest thing in the world.

Tom felt Raghnall's piercing gaze fall on him, and his languid polite air seemed to disappear. "Really, Tom? There's a lot more to you than meets the eye."

Tom wasn't sure whether to be insulted or flattered. Insulted, probably. Did he look like an idiot?

Before he could respond, Woodsmoke said, "Don't we all have hidden depths, Raghnall? Even you, I'm sure."

Tom suppressed a smirk by taking a big mouthful of food, watching Raghnall's response out of the corner of his eye.

Raghnall looked at Woodsmoke, a slow smile spreading across his face. "Indeed I do. It is possible, though, to eat well, sleep well, and generally live well, even with hidden depths, don't you think?"

"Absolutely," Woodsmoke said, raising his glass. "Here's to your excellent wine."

An unpleasant undercurrent seemed to have risen to the surface, and in an effort to submerge it again, Beansprout spoke. "Excuse me, Raghnall, but could you recommend a weapon maker tomorrow? I have a piece of dragon scale I would like making into something."

Raghnall held Woodsmoke's gaze for a second longer, then turned to Beansprout. "It would be a pleasure, my dear. And of course, Arthur will need a gem-maker."

"Ah, yes. My dragonyx. Your help would be much appreciated," Arthur said smoothly.

"It's quite a feat to kill a dragon."

Arthur must have decided that Raghnall had been baited enough. "And to enchant them too, I'm sure."

"I must admit the spell requires a lot of maintenance. It is not something every sorcerer could manage for so long, or so successfully. It both repels the dragons and provides a force of protection over the city and passes."

Raghnall's humour seemed to have returned, and he called for the last course. His servant appeared and disappeared in seconds, clearing the plates and returning with dessert. Raghnall continued, "Even you, Nimue, with your great powers, could not maintain this spell. Although I gather your powers are currently bound."

"Yes, courtesy of the Cervini shaman. He seemed to take exception to my putting their leader in a spell. And Nerian still carries my poppet," Nimue said before Arthur could explain, "and refuses to restore my powers. It seems I must wait for a while."

Why, thought Tom, did she just lie to Raghnall? Why wouldn't she want him to know Arthur carried her poppet? However, despite discrete glances across the table, no one corrected her lie, and she picked up her glass and took a delicate sip. "And yet," she continued, "a dragon did attack us today, despite your spell. I have a theory."

"Please, I would like to hear your thoughts on it," Raghnall said magnanimously, his tone of voice suggesting her opinion was the last thing he wanted.

"I think Excalibur called the dragon."

"Really?" He tapped his glass thoughtfully. "I have heard of your Excalibur, Arthur. May I see it?"

Arthur pulled Excalibur free of its scabbard and handed it, hilt first, to Raghnall. The light slid across the polished blade and Tom was sure he heard it whisper, like silk across a polished surface. Raghnall handled it gently and reverently, but his eyes were greedy, and he held it inches from his face, following its smooth lines and intricate engravings. "Take me up, and cast me away," he murmured before falling silent in contemplation.

"What?" asked Tom.

"It's what the writing on the sword says," Arthur explained, watching Raghnall.

"I hear it," Raghnall whispered. "It speaks of many things: its birth in the fires of the Forger of Light, snatches of song, of victory, death, blood, strange lands, broken promises, of belonging." Raghnall's eyes were now closed, and it seemed he barely breathed, so intense were his thoughts. Nimue leaned forward, listening closely. She glanced at Arthur and then back to Raghnall, her expression concerned. Finally, Raghnall opened his eyes, looking dazed, and his gaze moved around the table, finally settling on Arthur. "I think it is one of the most incredible weapons I have heard."

"I thought only dragons could hear that. How can you hear it?" Nimue asked, watching him intently.

Raghnall made an effort to shake off his otherworldly state. "The old royal houses of the fey have many diverse and special skills. And this is my skill, Nimue, didn't you know?"

"No, actually I didn't."

"It is why I collect such weapons. It is why I live here. I love their songs." Again he appeared distracted. As if he had said too much, he handed back Excalibur to Arthur. "Yes, it most certainly called the dragon. It is very powerful."

Arthur looked with renewed admiration at Excalibur and asked, "But you couldn't hear it before? Before you tried?"

"No," Raghnall admitted, "but it is a skill I have to switch on. Living here, surrounded by such things, I would go mad if I heard these songs all the time."

"Are we in danger here? Will Excalibur call the dragons into the Hollow?" Arthur asked, concerned.

"No. The spells around the city are much more powerful than on the mountain. You can sleep easy tonight." Raghnall's gaze fell to the sword again and there was a greed in it he couldn't quite hide. "But just to be sure, I can cast a spell of protection on your scabbard, if you wish?"

Arthur looked uncertain, and Raghnall added, "It would make your journey out of the Hollow much safer."

Arthur nodded. "All right."

Raghnall nodded to Nimue. "It is a spell you are familiar with." He took Arthur's scabbard and for a few minutes held his hand over it, muttering words unknown to Tom, until a blue light passed over the scabbard. "There, as long Excalibur is sheathed the dragons will not hear it."

Nimue nodded. "It's a good spell, Arthur."

As Arthur sheathed Excalibur, Woodsmoke said, "So you collect weapons, Raghnall?"

"Yes, I have a special room I keep them in. I will show you tomorrow if you like?"

Woodsmoke nodded. "Yes please."

"But perhaps before it becomes too late we should examine your dragonyx, Arthur?" Raghnall suggested, looking towards the wrapped jewel on the divan where it now lay. "Not many outside the Hollow know to take the heart."

"I would imagine it's not something you advertise, Raghnall?" Arthur said softly.

Raghnall didn't answer, and instead a ghost of a smile crossed his face.

Arthur picked up the dragonyx and put it on the table, gently removing its wrappings. It glowed in the soft candlelight, and just visible through the milky opacity of the jewel's outer shell they could see the ruby luminescence, the veins of gold and the black knot at its centre. It was hard to believe Arthur had cut it out of a dragon earlier, and that it had once been a living beating heart pulsing with blood.

Raghnall rose from his seat and stood over the dragonyx, staring at it intently. He examined it from every angle, before finally putting his hand on the stone and listening.

"One of the older dragons, I think," Raghnall murmured. "What colour was it?"

"Blue and green," Nimue said.

"And it was very big," Tom added.

"Mmm, maybe it was Viridain," Raghnall said thoughtfully. "Ah well, we shall soon see tomorrow, when we visit the Chamber of Transformation."

"The what?" Beansprout said.

"The place where the dragon is taken apart for its gold and jewels. I can assure you, it's fascinating. And then we will visit the gem-makers, where you will find, Arthur, that you will get a good price for your dragonyx."

Chapter 23 The Price of Dragons

The Chamber of Transformation was carved out of the rock deep beneath the left peak, and was accessed by a long tunnel that started in the town. It was rough hewn, long, low roofed and stiflingly hot. A central pit filled with flames lit up the cavern with a lurid glow, casting the faces of the goblins, trolls and fey who worked there into strange contorted shapes. The air rang with the sound of saws and hammers and the zing of metal on metal.

The dragon Arthur had slayed was spread on a large flat area of stone, where half a dozen goblins had already started to peel away its scaly skin and strip its veins and arteries of gold. Tom was forced to agree with Raghnall. As gory as it was, this was fascinating.

"I was right," Raghnall said, self-importantly. "This is Viridain. Or was."

"Do you name them all?" Tom asked.

"Only the ones we see most often. Although there are bigger dragons, this one was bold and caused many deaths over his long life. His hoard will be huge." Raghnall looked excited at the prospect of new gold. "And," he added quickly, "his hoard is not yours, Arthur. It belongs to the city."

"Don't worry," Arthur said. "I think I'll have enough gold."

"Do you know where his hoard is?" Beansprout asked.

"Not exactly, but I have a good idea." There was a speculative glint in Raghnall's eye.

Nimue muttered, "Of course you do."

Above the dragon's body was a series of wooden walkways, ropes and pulleys, and large buckets. Next to the body, running along the floor to the fire pit and other areas of the cave, were tracks carrying wheeled containers into which various parts of the dragon were placed.

The goblins had already made a lot of progress. Shiny gold sinews and what were once veins and arteries were already overflowing one container. With a shout and a mighty push, a goblin leapt onto the flat-bottomed trolley the container was on, escorting it to the edge of the fire pit. He leant on a bar which applied the brakes, and then, manipulating another switch, the cart tipped, sending the gold sliding over the edge.

Another goblin had started to fill a cart with the dragon's glittering scales, and yet another was loading what appeared to be the organs and viscera into a trolley destined for a different part of the cave. It was such a clinical operation that Tom felt repulsed.

"The process of transformation starts with the death of the dragon," Raghnall said. "The organs start to change from flesh to jewels, but we have found that the application of heat speeds up the process and improves the quality of the gems."

"So the whole dragon turns into gems?" Beansprout said.

"No. Not at all. There are parts that are quite unusable! But we are adept at getting the most out of them," Raghnall said smugly. "Of course, it has been quite some time since we have had a dragon to transform. They are notoriously difficult to kill." He looked at Arthur with begrudging admiration.

Tom stepped away from Raghnall and followed one of the tracks to the fire pit, curious to see where the gold went.

The pit descended into the rock far deeper than he'd imagined. Huge cauldrons were suspended over the fire, surrounded by metal walkways on which stood more goblins, stirring the pots with huge wooden paddles. They must be immune to the heat, thought Tom. And surely the metal walkways should burn and melt? More tracks led to another area, where the molten metals were being poured into moulds to create small ingots.

The others appeared next to him. "I have cast a protective spell over the walkways," said Raghnall, "to prevent the conduction of heat. As for the goblins, they enjoy it!"

"All this is for one dragon?" Woodsmoke asked.

"Oh no. The melting of precious metals is a continual process here. We process gold from dragon hoards, and from the rich seams of metal found beneath the mountain. At the moment, though, this is all for Viridain, so we can calculate Arthur's bounty." He looked a little annoyed at the prospect of wealth going somewhere other than the city.

"I think I need fresh air," Brenna said suddenly, a look of distaste flashing across her face.

"Yes, me too," Beansprout agreed. "I'm hot."

The pair turned and headed towards the cave entrance.

"But I was going to show you the gem preparation!" Raghnall called, a look of anguish on his face.

"I think the heat is getting to us," said Woodsmoke, also turning to leave. "We'll see you back at the entrance." He slapped Raghnall unceremoniously on the shoulder before following Brenna and Beansprout.

"It's just me, Nimue and Tom, then," Arthur said. Tom half wished he could leave too, but Arthur gave him a quick look that compelled him to stay.

"Excellent. I'm so glad you're not squeamish," Raghnall said. He turned with a flourish and headed to the rear of the cave.

"I feel we should humour him, Tom," Arthur whispered with a wink and a smirk, and then set off after Raghnall.

Arthur rarely humoured anyone, Tom thought. What was he up to?

An hour later they found the others enjoying a cool drink on the terrace of a restaurant close to the entrance. Beansprout waved to draw their attention, and they weaved through the crowds to join them.

"Would you at least like to see the gem-makers' workshops?" Raghnall asked. He gestured across the green open space in front of them to a row of glittering shop fronts.

"Is that where I can get Viridain's scale polished up?" Beansprout said.

"Of course. And where the dragonyx can be weighed, polished and priced," he said with a nod to Arthur.

Raghnall was enjoying this, Tom thought, showing off the city and its citizens' skills. And why not? The city was beautiful, gilded and sleek. The whole place gleamed, the food was sumptuous, and the drinks were delicious. He felt pampered and rested, especially after weeks on the road. The atmosphere of success and satisfaction was addictive. He just wished he felt more relaxed here. This wasn't something he was used to, unlike Arthur. It was a strange thing to say, but Tom thought Arthur looked bigger. He seemed to have grown into himself. He was more self-assured – the promise of wealth seemed to invigorate him.

"Come on then," Arthur said after they'd finished their drinks. "Let's head to the gem-makers."

They stopped first at a small shop with a glittering array of polished scales in its window. The scales had been skilfully turned into jewellery, sword and dagger hilts, scabbards, and items Tom didn't even recognise. Inside the shop were gleaming metal cabinets displaying more polished scales. A fey bustled out of the door from the rear of the shop and was about to launch into his sales pitch when he saw Raghnall. His face froze for a fraction of a second, his eyes wide. Quickly recovering, he beamed ingratiatingly. "What a pleasure, Raghnall, it's been too long."

After a brief exchange of pleasantries, Raghnall introduced them, and then said, "Beansprout, please show him your scale."

She handed it over, and the conversation turned to business. The fey narrowed his eyes, pulled out a small magnifying glass and proceeded to examine the scale minutely. He then started on requirements, design, practicalities, time, and finally price – which was exorbitant. Clearly, whatever issues he had with Raghnall did not interrupt business. Raghnall bartered, Beansprout looked pale, Nimue questioned, but Arthur finished it all by naming a final price and declaring he would pay as a gift for Beansprout.

With a sigh of relief, Tom trailed out of the shop after them, to where Brenna and Woodsmoke waited in the sun, having long run out of patience during bargaining.

"Pleased, Beansprout?" Arthur asked, smiling.

"Well yes, but Arthur – I didn't expect you to pay!"

"My treat," he announced magnanimously. "And besides, at those prices it would have sat in your pack forever."

"True," Beansprout said, embarrassed. "It was very expensive!"

They followed Raghnall further along the row of expensive shops until they came to the largest and most ostentatious. It was a blaze of gold and glittering gems. Even Woodsmoke looked impressed.

Raghnall only had to mention dragonyx and a small silence fell across the handful of fey in the shop, both sellers and buyers. With hushed ceremony, the oldest and most imperious fey, who had a shock of rich purple hair and wore a black silk jacket, stepped from behind the long bronze-topped counter and said, "I have heard of the slaying of Viridain. Who has slain the dragon?"

Arthur stepped forward introducing himself, and the shop owner shook his hand vigorously. "Arshok. I am honoured to meet you. Please follow me to our salon, where I will offer refreshments while we negotiate." He glanced at Raghnall and added, "Perhaps just you and Arthur?"

Standing next to Nimue, Tom heard her whisper to Arthur, "Have you any idea of what it's worth?"

Arthur shook his head. "Not really."

"Then I suggest you let me come too," she said, raising an eyebrow.

Arthur turned to where the owner and Raghnall waited expectantly and said, "Nimue will join us." Raghnall flashed a brief discomforted smile as Arshok opened a richly embellished gold door.

Woodsmoke called to Arthur, "We won't wait, see you later."

Arthur nodded his agreement and stepped into the room beyond. Tom caught a glimpse of silks and brocades, and then the door thudded shut.

"Come on," Woodsmoke said. "Let's see what else there is, other than jewellery shops. If this is where they make weapons, I want to see some." He gave the others a broad grin. "Besides, I need a break from Raghnall."

Woodsmoke led the way across the city, along broad boulevards and down tiny passageways, taking a circuitous route so they could see the city better. The beautiful buildings they passed were all manner of shapes and sizes, and while some were clearly for the town merchants, there appeared to be no poorer rundown areas at all. Eventually they came to an indoor market beside the lake. It was sprawled across a large area, with several entrances. Woodsmoke headed for the nearest one, and they plunged into the warren of stalls.

They were immediately surrounded by the loud hum of voices and jostling crowds that packed the small lanes between the shops. The bright glare of the day was shut out, replaced by the airless glitter of candles and lanterns, and the occasional chink of sunlight filtering in through the open entrances. The stall owners called to them constantly.

"Come and see the best silks this side of the Sky Meadows!"

"Come, madam, come taste the best spices in the market!"

"Sir, sir, this way for the best knives and best deals!"

The choice of wares and the dazzling displays mesmerised Tom. He had never been in such a place before; the markets of Holloway's Meet were pedestrian and grey in comparison. Beansprout agreed. "Tom, this place is brilliant! So much stuff!"

Brenna laughed. "Take your time, and if you buy anything, make sure to haggle. We'll see you in the weapons section." And she hurried into the sea of bodies to catch up with Woodsmoke.

As Tom and Beansprout drifted down the alleys, they realised the market was divided into distinct areas. There was a section of clothing, silks, scarves and cloaks, then silverware, home wares, food, jewellery, shoes, travel supplies, magic amulets, glassware, lamps, rugs, books, and weapons. The choice was endless and the prices much cheaper than in the shops they had passed. They quickly lost track of time, meandering through the tiny lanes and buying all manner of trinkets, clothes and books.

"I think we should get a move on, Tom," Beansprout said at last, "before Woodsmoke runs out of patience."

"He's looking at weapons, he could be there all day!" Tom said.

They eventually stumbled upon the weapons quarter. The choice of weapons was vast. There were spears, axes, longbows, arrows, shields, helmets, armour, and all manner of swords and knives. The stalls spread into a central courtyard where a series of targets had been set up to test the weapons. They found Woodsmoke and Brenna by the stalls selling daggers, throwing-knives and swords. Brenna was testing the balance of a pack of throwing-knives, carefully hefting each one in her hands.

"New weapons, Brenna?" Tom asked, looking at the knives she was examining.

"I used to have a set of knives many years ago," she said, smiling at the memory. "And then I lost them, one after another. I have no idea how. I was thinking of getting some more."

"And these," Woodsmoke said, picking one up, "are very nice." He raised it to eye level, admiring its shape.

"The finest dragon metals have been combined to maximise weight, strength and longevity," the stall owner, a broad squat dwarf, explained. "Platinum, gold and dragonium. And the inlaid gems on the handles are black opals and pearls."

"Wow," Beansprout said, extending her hand. "May I?"

Brenna passed her a knife to examine, and said to the dwarf, "I like the metals, but not the jewels."

The dwarf immediately produced another knife, virtually identical but with a carved bone handle. "Dragon bone, hardened in the fires of the Djinn," he grunted.

"Better," Brenna said, examining it closely. She turned, eyed up the targets and threw the knife. The wooden targets were fashioned into a variety of creatures, including boar, dragons, trolls, and sprites. The knife sank deep into the eye of a sprite, and Tom was immediately reminded of their encounter with them in Finnlugh's Under-Palace and the Aerie.

"You seem to have kept your aim, Brenna," Tom said, impressed.

She smiled. "Not bad – I was aiming for his forehead." She went to retrieve the knife.

"He'd still be dead," Tom said. "Is it hard to learn?" Another skill to add to his growing sword skills would be good.

"Not really, you just need lots of practice," Brenna told him. "I'll teach you."

"Can you throw knives, Woodsmoke?" Tom asked.

"Of course I can!" he snorted while Brenna rolled her eyes. "But I prefer my bow and sword. It's a good skill for you to learn, though. I'm sure this good dwarf has plenty of cheaper knives for you to practise with."

While Brenna negotiated a price for her set of knives, Woodsmoke helped Tom choose.

"Have you bought anything, Woodsmoke?" Beansprout asked.

"New arrows, fletches, and a sharpening stone. Speaking of which, we should get you some more arrows." He pointed to the stalls on the far side of the courtyard.

After Tom and Brenna paid, they made their way over to the arrow stalls. Choosing one at random, they entered the dim interior. Concentrating on making their choice, Tom suddenly became aware of someone looming close beside Woodsmoke. The faerie was tall, with fine features and high cheekbones, his hair long and fair with plaits and beads running through it. He leant in and said something in Woodsmoke's ear. Woodsmoke whipped round, his hand moving to his dagger. Subconsciously, Tom reached for his sword too, wondering briefly where Brenna was. But then Woodsmoke laughed, relief etched across his face.

"Bloodmoon, you nearly had my dagger in your stomach! What brings you to the Hollow?"

"Hunting, my friend."

"Hunting what?" Woodsmoke asked.

He grinned. "That should be discussed over a drink. What are you doing so far from home?"

"Also hunting, of a sort."

"Indeed?" He caught sight of Tom and Beansprout looking on curiously. "Humans. Are they with you?"

"They are. And a lot of trouble they cause too. Tom, Beansprout – Bloodmoon," he said. "Many things have happened since I last saw you."

Bloodmoon shook their hands. "No Brenna?"

"Oh, she's here, somewhere. Give us half an hour and we'll see you at the Dragon's Tale, if you've time?"

"Always. Soon, then," Bloodmoon said, and he disappeared back into the crowd.

"Who's he?" Tom asked.

"My cousin. Come, Beansprout, let's get your arrows, and then we'll find Brenna and see what Bloodmoon is hunting."

Chapter 24 Objects of Desire

The Dragon's Tale was a very old inn, lacking the ostentatious decorations of the rest of the city, although its wooden structure was decorated with the finest carvings. Its customers were mainly those visiting the market and the stall owners, and it served cheap hearty fare.

Bloodmoon joined them shortly after they sat down in a quiet corner. He greeted Brenna with an enormous kiss that had her blushing. "Bloodmoon!" she exclaimed breathlessly. "What was that for?"

"I haven't seen you in a long time," he said, grinning. "And when you're the Queen of Aeriken I won't be able to get away with that."

"You're such a show-off," Woodsmoke said. "Just sit down and tell us what you're up to. Nothing good, I presume?"

Bloodmoon sat down, placing an enormous tankard of frothing beer on the table next to his parcel. He took a long sip while the others watched him expectantly, and then said, "I'm tracking a lamia."

"What on earth for?" Woodsmoke asked, alarmed. "Is there one in Dragon's Hollow?"

"Not in the city, but I think she's on the mountain. I've been following her for weeks. She moves very quickly."

"Why follow her though?" Brenna asked.

"A few weeks ago she attacked and killed the daughter of the Lady of the Four Hills. She has employed me to kill the lamia." He shrugged at their puzzled faces. "I was at a loose end. And she's paying me in tear-diamonds."

"Oh, that explains it," Woodsmoke said.

Beansprout looked confused. "At the risk of sounding stupid, what's a lamia, and what's a tear-diamond?"

"A lamia is a blood-sucking snake that takes the guise of a beautiful lady. They usually feed on the blood of children, but when they're hungry they'll eat anything," Bloodmoon explained. "And tear-diamonds are the most beautiful diamonds anywhere, formed from the tears of Djinn. And as anyone knows, Djinn rarely cry. I have had an advance." He pulled a small leather pouch from around his neck and took out two small tear-shaped diamonds that dazzled, even in the dim light of the tavern.

"But they're blue!" Tom said.

"Not all diamonds are white, and these will fetch me a good price, which is good because I need to buy a sword of pure dragonium. That's the only metal known to kill a lamia. And I only know that," he added, "because I thought I'd killed her. Then her head grew back and I had to make a tactical retreat. Fortunately, a very nice satyr in the Meet told me the trick. So here I am, in the best place to get a pure dragonium sword. I've spent the morning bargaining. Your turn."

Bloodmoon sipped his beer while Woodsmoke told him of their hunt. As he listened, Tom compared Bloodmoon to Woodsmoke and decided they were very different. Woodsmoke had a quiet watchfulness about him, but Bloodmoon was all words.

When Woodsmoke reached the end of his tale, Bloodmoon said, "So you're travelling with Arturus! And searching for Merlin! You keep interesting company these days."

"You've heard the name?" Tom asked, suddenly paying attention. "Nimue called him that."

"One of Arthur's old names, I believe. The name some of the older fey call him. That or Artaius, The Bear King of Kernow."

"Where's Kernow?" Tom said, even more confused.

"I believe it is the name of an old kingdom in Britain."

Tom thought of the stories he'd read, and the name Arthur had called himself only the other day. "He called himself the Boar of Cornwall, not bear."

"I have no idea where the name came from, I just know it exists." Bloodmoon shrugged, giving Tom a wry smile.

"I forgot you had Fahey's ear for tales," Woodsmoke said.

"Does Arthur still carry Excalibur?" Bloodmoon asked.

"Of course."

"And you're staying with Raghnall?"

"Yes, why?"

"I have heard many things about Raghnall. Particularly regarding his collection of ancient magical weapons. Be careful while you stay with him."

Brenna reassured him. "Don't worry, we will. Arthur should have finished his business today, so hopefully we leave soon."

"Ah! The dragonyx?"

Woodsmoke laughed. "News does travel quickly here."

"I must go," Bloodmoon said, finishing his drink. "I have a sword to buy and a lamia to track. Safe travels." After a flurry of handshakes and hugs, he left.

When they arrived at the House of the Beloved late that afternoon, they found Arthur on the balcony with Nimue.

"How did you get on, Arthur?" Tom asked, helping himself to a drink.

"Very well! The dragonyx has gone and now I am rich. I've kept some money, the rest is in The Lair, as they call their banking house. And it's all thanks to Nimue."

"It was the least I could do." She was sitting on the divan again, her green eyes glinting.

"Making amends for your evil deeds?" Woodsmoke said, flinging himself in a chair.

Nimue glared at him. "You could say that. Or you could say I'm happy to help an old friend."

"Whatever you call it," Arthur said, lowering his voice, "I would have got far less without Nimue. I hate to say it, but I think Raghnall was working with Arshok to give me less money, no doubt for his own cut of the future profits. I'm beginning to hate the man."

"If you've finished business, maybe we should leave sooner rather than later, Arthur," Brenna suggested. "I don't trust Raghnall."

"No, nor I. But I don't want to upset him either. I suggested we might leave tomorrow and he looked very offended. He wants to show us the weapons room, was quite insistent in fact. Tomorrow he has to attend an important business meeting with the city leaders. He says he can't miss it – something about trade rights with the sylphs. He'll show us his collection when he returns, so I've agreed we'll stay one more day. At first I was hoping to stay longer, but as much as I like the city I do not wish to stay here," he said, gesturing to Raghnall's house. "And I want to see Merlin. I'm worried about him."

"Why can't we see the weapons room tonight?" Brenna asked. She had taken her new knives out and examined them in the light as she spoke.

Nimue laughed dryly, and broke into an impression of Raghnall. "Oh no, tonight I must ensure it is ready for you. I couldn't bear for you to see it other than perfect."

Brenna narrowed her eyes. "Really?"

Nimue's criticism of Raghnall reminded Tom of their conversation the previous night. "Why didn't you want Raghnall to know Arthur has your poppet, Nimue?"

"Because I don't like being too honest with him, Tom." She smiled coyly.

"But what was your old argument about Avalon?" said Tom.

"You do pay attention, don't you?" she said, staring at him. "He doesn't like that Avalon has restricted access. It's a powerful place, and he thinks its powers should be available to all. He's wrong."

She sipped her drink and fell quiet, and realising this was the only answer he would get, Tom turned to Beansprout. "And what about your dragon scale?"

"Raghnall has influence," she said, "so it will be ready tomorrow. We can collect it when I do more shopping." She grinned. "At least we'll have time for that."

They headed back to their rooms. Tom was so tired he dozed for a while on his bed. When he woke the bath was again ready, the water scented and steaming with towels ready at the side. He could easily grow used to this, and wished they were staying longer. But, like the others, he found it hard to feel comfortable with Raghnall. And he wanted to see Merlin again. With the excitement of the past few days, he'd pushed him to the back of his mind, but now he wondered how Merlin would be. Or whether he would even agree to see them at all.

The next morning, while the others headed into the city, Tom and Woodsmoke went to check on the horses. As they crossed the large walled courtyard where the stables were located, Woodsmoke glanced over to an archway, through which they could see a track leading behind the stables and on towards the mountain.

"Interesting. I wonder where that goes?" Woodsmoke murmured.

They found the horses well fed and groomed, although there were no servants in sight.

Woodsmoke was pleased. "At least the horses are being looked after, but this place is creepier than Enisled. There, there, Farlight," he whispered to his horse as she nudged him. "I think you need some exercise." He started to saddle her.

"Where are you going?" Tom asked.

He tossed Tom his saddle. "I think you mean 'we'. We're going to check out that path. Midnight needs a run too."

Tom quickly prepared his horse, fumbling with the straps, and followed Woodsmoke onto the track. He stood awkwardly for a few seconds, conscious of all the windows looking down on him, and wondered who might be watching, before nudging Midnight onwards.

"Should we be on this path?" Tom asked, worried. "We could get into trouble."

"It's just a road, Tom. I'm sure Raghnall won't mind."

Very quickly the road became rutted and muddy, and then there was a tangle of branches blocking the way forward.

"It's a dead end," Tom said, frustrated, about to turn around.

"Wait." Woodsmoke slipped off his horse, pushed through the undergrowth and disappeared. For a few seconds Tom waited alone, listening to cracking branches and the call of a bird, and then Woodsmoke was back, grinning broadly.

"It's just a ruse, Tom." He grabbed Farlight's reins and pushed back through the undergrowth.

Tom quickly followed, pulling a reluctant Midnight behind him. For a few minutes he battled through the vegetation, and then he was through to the other side. Ahead of him a smooth, well-maintained road ran through a densely wooded area, snaking away from the house and the city and up the slopes of the mountain.

"I'm pretty sure Raghnall wouldn't like us being here," Tom said, looking around him.

Woodsmoke smirked. "Well we must make sure he doesn't know."

The road rose in a gentle incline until eventually the trees thinned and they could see the city glittering on the valley floor. After a few more minutes the path turned to follow the contours of the mountain, clinging tightly to its side, but before long they came to a halt. The road was again blocked, this time by a massive landslide.

"I think this has been blocked by magic, Tom. It seems to me the path is too well maintained to end here. But there's nothing we can do about it now. We'd better head back."

Chapter 25 Under Seven Moons

They stood in front of the weapons room, gathered together in anticipation. The room was sealed by a door covered in runes and sigils, and Raghnall stood before it, murmuring incantations. Suddenly a seam appeared down the centre and the large door split into two. It opened with a quiet hiss, swinging back into blackness. Raghnall stepped inside, closely followed by the others.

Immediately a soft low light illuminated the room. It came from seven silvery moons hanging beneath a vaulted ceiling – moons that ranged from a tiny sliver of a crescent, to full and then waxing. The room had been transformed into a forest glade. Objects were displayed around the glade on pedestals, and as Raghnall approached the closest, a broad ray of moonlight illuminated it clearly and writing appeared in the air: Brionac. The weapon was a large spear, cradled in a silver hand on top of wooden pedestal, the moonlight glinting off its sharp tip.

"Behold," Raghnall said portentously, "Brionac, the spear of Lugh."

"One of the ancient fey kings of Ireland," Arthur said. "He was myth in my time. How do you have this?"

Raghnall smiled. "I have my ways."

"Brionac is supposedly impossible to overcome," Arthur mused.

"All of the weapons here have true magical properties," Raghnall told them. "They may belong to history, but their powers are real."

Woodsmoke stepped forward to look at it closely. "May I?" he said, indicating he wanted to pick it up.

Raghnall hesitated for a second, then said, "Of course."

Woodsmoke reached forward to take the spear as the silver hand released it. He hefted it as if to throw it. "It's perfect."

Arthur had already turned away to the rest of the objects, and the others split up and drifted around the glade. Tom headed to a sword lying lengthways, cradled in two hands on a long pedestal. He grasped the hilt and pulled it from the scabbard. Immediately a deep voice started speaking words he couldn't understand.

Tom looked around, confused, wondering where the voice was coming from, before realising it was coming from the sword. He lifted the sword to his ear, as if that would help him translate it.

"It is called Orna. It's the sword of King Tethra," Raghnall said from behind him. "Once unsheathed it recounts all its deeds."

"Why can't I understand it?" Tom asked.

"Because it speaks in an old language not used for many years." Raghnall turned to where Beansprout stood in front of armour magically suspended, as if over an invisible body. "The armour of the Elven King Sorcha, Wolf Lord of the North," he called. "It repels all blades. None can pierce it."

Tom replaced Orna in its scabbard and joined Brenna, who was picking up a bow. It seemed to be made of the flimsiest material, the wood delicate and the bow string so fine as to be almost invisible.

"Artemis's Bow!" she exclaimed. She turned to Tom. "Do you think all this is real? I wouldn't put it past him to do this just to impress us."

"I don't think the lock would be so elaborate if they weren't real," he replied.

Tom continued to wander around the glade, sometimes losing sight of the others behind the trees. Raghnall's collection contained bows, spears, swords, helmets, rings of enchantment, gemstones, and even a silver saddle. Then he heard Arthur shout, "Raghnall! Is this a joke?"

Tom found Arthur standing before a collection of weapons in a clearing. On a large flat rock were a dagger, a helmet, a spear and a shield, and placed within the rock, the blade buried half way, was a sword.

Raghnall joined Arthur, smiling slyly. "No. Not a joke. I thought you'd be pleased?"

"How could I be pleased to see my own weapons displayed? And that!" Arthur pointed at the sword.

"What do you mean, your weapons?" Tom asked. The others joined them, concern on their faces.

It was Nimue who spoke first. "Clarent – The Sword of Peace." She turned to Raghnall, frowning. "What incredibly bad taste, Raghnall."

Raghnall's eyes flashed. "It is a sword of great beauty, whatever it may have done."

"It almost killed me!" Arthur exclaimed angrily.

"What?" Beansprout said.

"Clarent was my ceremonial sword, never meant for combat," Arthur explained. "Morgan stole it and gave it to Mordred. It was the sword he used in the Battle of Camlann."

"And the other weapons?" Woodsmoke asked.

"Priwen, my shield; Goswhit, my helmet; Carnwennan, my dagger; and Rhongomiant, my spear." Arthur rounded on Raghnall. "Are you planning to return them to me?"

"No. They are mine now. I obtained them lawfully, presuming you dead." He faced Arthur, implacable, his eyes drifting to Excalibur, Arthur's hand now clutching the hilt.

"You knew I wasn't dead, Raghnall. And as I am now standing before you, very much alive, I'd like my weapons back. Or are you wanting to add Excalibur to your collection?" A dangerous icy tone had entered his voice.

"Well, it would enhance my collection," he said, with smile that didn't quite reach his eyes. "Would you like to sell it?"

"No, I would not!" Arthur yelled, pulling Excalibur out of its scabbard.

"A shame then. I had hoped not to do this, you have been such interesting guests." Raghnall made the briefest of gestures and stepped back half a pace. A flash of light enveloped him, just as Arthur swung Excalibur at his head, so swiftly that Tom barely saw it. At the same time, Woodsmoke lifted Brionac and hurled it at Raghnall.

There was a thunk as Raghnall's head hit the floor and rolled to Arthur's feet. His body had disappeared, along with Brionac.

A sharp intake of breath was followed by a stunned silence as everybody looked at Raghnall's head and then at Arthur. Within seconds the forest glade and the seven moons began to fade, and through the vanishing illusion they saw the walls start to appear.

Nimue looked quizzically at Arthur. "I'm not sure that was a good idea."

"I think it was. He was about to do something treacherous, and I've had enough of him. Woodsmoke obviously agreed. I will not be threatened by a pompous idiot, who for the second time today has tried to steal from me."

Tom felt a wave of nausea wash over him as Raghnall's grinning rictus stared up at them. Killing a dragon was one thing, but this ... He looked at Beansprout and was relieved to find she looked as bad as he felt.

"Yes, but Arthur," Nimue continued, "Raghnall was the only one keeping the dragons away from the city."

Arthur stuttered as understanding dawned. "O-Oh, I'd forgotten that ..."

"How long have we got?" Woodsmoke asked, also looking a little sheepish.

"I have no idea, but it won't be long. Arthur, I think it's time you unbound my poppet."

"Can you continue the spell?" Beansprout asked.

"I can't continue it. With his death the spell has broken. But I can make a new one. I think."

"You think?" Woodsmoke said, incredulous.

"As he boasted, it is a powerful spell, and I don't know it."

Arthur thrust Excalibur at Tom and started searching his pockets furiously. "I thought I'd put it in my inside pocket." His earlier composure had disappeared.

"I'll go and see what's happening." Brenna swiftly changed form and flew out of the room.

"They can't possibly be here already!" Tom said, desperately hoping he was right. How could they fight half a dozen dragons or more?

"Arthur?" pressed Nimue.

"I've got it!" He produced the poppet with a flourish and thrust it at Nimue. "Here, do whatever you have to!"

As it touched her hands it immediately sizzled. Nimue cursed and dropped the poppet on to the floor. "Nerian didn't trust me to even hold it! You will have to do it, Arthur."

Arthur snatched it up, annoyed. "What do I do?"

"Unwind the cord that wraps it. Gently."

He hesitated for a second and looked at her questioningly.

"You can trust me, Arthur. And besides, what choice do you have?"

"That's what worries me," he muttered.

In a few seconds the cord came free, and Nimue took it from him. She clicked her fingers and the cord turned to ash. "Excellent. Now we have to find where Raghnall performed the spell."

"Why does that matter?" Beansprout asked.

"Because you can guarantee that wherever he did it will be the best place."

"We'd better start looking then," Arthur said. He retrieved Excalibur from Tom and said to Woodsmoke, "Grab weapons! Anything you think will be useful. I will take what is rightfully mine." He put his dagger in his belt, his shield over his arm, his helmet on his head, and then grabbed his spear.

Tom looked at him, slightly stunned.

"What's the matter, Tom?"

"You look very ..." he struggled for words, "kingly, I suppose. You don't want the sword then?"

"No," he said, narrowing his eyes at Clarent. "That can stay here. But I saw something for you, Tom. He strode across to another sword. "Galatine."

"What?" Tom asked, confused.

"Take it. It was Sir Gawain's sword, given to him by Vivian." He smiled. "It is the sister sword to Excalibur, and Gawain was my nephew, and one of my bravest and most loyal knights. He also died because of Mordred."

"Arthur, I can't take it," Tom stuttered, overawed as another piece of the ancient past appeared before him.

"Yes you can. You're my family and I want you to have it."

Tom gazed at Galatine, speechless.

"Tom, take it. We haven't got all day," Arthur said softly.

Tom felt a sudden tightness in his chest that had nothing to do with dragons, and he took the sword from Arthur, his arms dropping beneath its weight. "Thank you."

"And for you—" Woodsmoke hurried over to Beansprout, carrying a bow. "The Fail-not. Tristan's bow, I believe. This should help your aim."

Beansprout took the bow from Woodsmoke. "Thanks, but who's Tristan?"

"Another of my contemporaries," Arthur said. "I think Raghnall had a slight obsession with me. Something else I must discuss with Vivian."

As he finished speaking, Brenna flew into the room.

"How bad is it?" Nimue asked.

"At the moment, nothing seems to be happening. I can't see any dragons, but it won't be long before they realise they can access the city. Once the dragons attack, Magen and the guard will realise something has happened to the spell, and to Magen's father."

Arthur groaned. "I'd forgotten about Magen too."

"I've found the rest of Raghnall's body," Brenna continued. "He didn't go far – just outside the doors. Brionac is embedded in his chest. And to make matters worse, it will be dark soon."

"What are we going to do about leaving?" Woodsmoke asked. "We're running out of time. If we don't leave soon, we could be stuck here for days if the pass is blocked by dragons. Or if they attack the city. Unless we move tonight." He quickly explained about the route that seemed to lead up higher over the mountain, bypassing the lower road. "And now Raghnall is dead, whatever magic was blocking his private road will have gone."

"If it was magic," Tom pointed out.

Brenna looked appalled. "But we can't abandon the city; everyone will die!"

"I'm not suggesting we abandon it," Woodsmoke said. "You can help Nimue start the spell. If we can only protect the city, that's better than nothing. The dragons can squat on the pass all they want as long as the city is safe."

"I agree," Nimue said. "As long as I can protect the city. So you need to go, quickly, before the mountains are full of dragons. Unless of course you want to stay, Arthur?"

Arthur looked at the floor and then at Nimue. "I need to see Merlin. But Woodsmoke's right. If we miss our chance today, we may be stuck here for days. Or even weeks. But," he added, "I don't want to see the city fall and people die. Or you. Will you be all right if we go?"

"I'm sure I can do the spell," she reassured him, "but I need to find where Raghnall performed it."

"I noticed something on the flat roof," Brenna said. "There seemed to be some kind of apparatus up there, and markings I couldn't decipher."

"That must be it," Nimue said, and she whirled around and ran for the door.

"I'll lead the way," Brenna said, and returning to bird form she flew ahead. Beansprout ran after her, Fail-not under her arm.

Arthur turned to Woodsmoke and Tom. "I suppose that leaves us with saddling the horses."

Chapter 26 Flight from the Hollow

Tom hurriedly finished packing. Hoisting the pack over his shoulder, he took one last long look at the bed, already missing it, and then headed to Beansprout's room and packed up her gear, hoping he hadn't missed anything.

Woodsmoke had already grabbed his own bags, and Brenna's, and had gone to saddle the horses with Arthur. Tom wandered to the window and looked out over the city below. It shone with lights, and Tom wondered if the fey had any idea that the spell had gone. Should they warn them? And if so, how? He looked up and thought he could just make out movement. A darker blackness on the night sky. Was that a dragon?

A movement closer to the house caught his eye. Magen and several dragon guards were heading towards them. He needed to warn the others.

Swinging a pack around each shoulder he headed onto the shadowy landing, partially lit from the city lights. The house felt eerily quiet. Just before he reached the back stairs, a figure stepped out of the shadows in front of him. He stopped and pulled Galatine free of its scabbard as the servant's voice spoke out of the darkness. "What have you done to Raghnall?"

"I haven't done anything!"

Tom's breath was knocked out of him as the servant jumped on him, wrestling him to the ground. Tom's right arm, holding Galatine, was pinned on the floor as the fey straddled his chest, his face inches from Tom's. "Is he dead?"

Gripping the sword tightly, Tom said, "Yes. Arthur killed him. But he was trying to—"

"Do you know what you've done?" the servant howled, spittle flying into Tom's face. "You have killed us all! The dragons are coming!"

The pale light showed the servant's face twisted in anger, his eyes as black as coal.

"But Nimue is—" Tom gasped. But he couldn't finish because the servant's strong hands closed around his throat and squeezed tightly.

Rather than release his sword, Tom desperately tried to get his left hand under the servant's, but he was gripping so tightly it was impossible. Instinctively he did the next best thing and punched him hard, again and again in the side of his head. The servant sprawled across the floor, and Tom rolled awkwardly, impeded by the packs on his shoulders. Still unable to free his right arm, Tom raised his right knee as high as he could and kicked the servant hard in the chest, pulling his sword free. Before Tom could get to his feet the servant launched himself again and Tom raised Galatine and jabbed forward, immediately finding flesh as the momentum of the servant pushed him down the blade, pinning Tom to the ground again.

For a few seconds Tom could hear nothing except the gurgle of blood in the servant's throat, and then he fell silent, his body limp and heavy. Tom wriggled and pushed until he could lever the servant off him, and then dragged himself to his feet.

He had killed someone. Again. Like when he was helping Arthur back in Aeriken. But, he reminded himself, the servant had been trying to kill him. He dusted himself off, and bending down, wiped the blade clean of blood on the servant's clothes, then ran down the stairs to the courtyard.

Tom found Arthur and Woodsmoke in the stables, talking quietly in the lamplight.

"A servant just attacked me," he announced, as he stepped through the door.

"What?" Woodsmoke pulled Tom into the light. "Are you all right?" He looked him up and down, searching for wounds.

"I'm fine, apart from a sore throat." He showed them his bruised neck. "But I've killed him."

"What happened?" Arthur asked.

"He ambushed me in the corridor. He was furious that Raghnall was dead, and then announced the dragons were coming. Like I didn't know!"

A proud look crossed Arthur's face. "Well done, Tom. I knew your fighting skills were improving."

Tom hadn't the heart to tell him it was more by accident than design. "Arthur, I think a dragon is already overhead, and Magen and the Dragon Guards are close. They're coming here."

"Just what I need," grumbled Arthur. "How many guards?"

Tom shrugged. "Five or six."

"Magen wasn't fond of his father," Woodsmoke reminded Arthur.

"No, but he was still his father. Tom, go and tell Beansprout and Brenna to get a move on. Woodsmoke, let's meet Magen at the gates to the house."

Nimue and the others were on a large flat area of the roof, set in the middle of several different-sized domes. It had taken Tom a few minutes to find them in the vast space, especially as he had to navigate around what appeared to be very large crossbows, aiming into the skies.

Nimue was pacing around a large intricate diagram inlaid on the roof in marble, gold and gems. Three small braziers flickering with firelight faintly illuminated the space. Beansprout watched Nimue, and Brenna leant against one of the giant crossbows, watching the sky.

Tom followed her gaze. *Crap*. There *was* a dragon circling overhead.

"How long's that been there?" he asked Brenna.

"It arrived just after we got up here. And," she turned and pointed, "there's another one. Any minute now they'll realise they can reach the city."

"Should we try and shoot it?" He nodded at the crossbow.

"I really don't want to draw attention to ourselves."

"Oh. Yes. You're probably right." He turned to Beansprout. "Are you nearly ready? Arthur said we have to go."

"No! We're not even close," Beansprout shot back impatiently. "We need to work out what this diagram means."

"I can understand most of it," Nimue said. "Maybe we could ask the servant, he must know." She looked up briefly. "Tom, can you go and find him?"

Tom swallowed. "Unfortunately not. He's dead."

"How?" Beansprout asked.

"He attacked me and I accidentally killed him."

Beansprout fell silent and looked at him with an expression that made him feel very uncomfortable, but Nimue glanced up once more towards the dragons and went back to pacing around the circle. "Let's hope I can work it out without him," she said.

Tom shuffled, feeling guilty. "Beansprout, are you coming?"

"Are you insane? You heard Nimue. The spell isn't done yet!"

"But Arthur said–"

"I don't care what Arthur said. We're not ready!"

"We can't leave Nimue alone, Tom," Brenna agreed.

Before Tom had a chance to respond, Nimue shouted, "*Yes!* Oh that's clever." She looked up to find the others looking at her expectantly. "It is clever. But I don't think I can do it alone. Not yet, anyway. And it's going to take a while."

"What do you mean?" Tom asked, confused.

"It's complicated. I'll need help."

"I'll stay," Beansprout said immediately.

"So will I," Brenna added.

Now Tom was even more confused. "What do you mean, you'll stay."

Beansprout looked at him as if he was child, and repeated slowly, "I will stay to help Nimue. So will Brenna. Do you understand?"

"Thank you for your sarcasm, Beansprout," Tom said, eyes narrowing. "So, you're not coming? At all? I thought you wanted to meet Merlin?"

"This is more important than Merlin."

"That's if you want a city to come back to," Nimue said. "And Tom, tell Arthur I will be able to protect the passes eventually, but not for the next few days."

Tom pulled Beansprout aside. "Are you sure you want to do this?" He nodded at Nimue. "Do you trust her?"

"Yes. Completely." Beansprout hugged him. "Now go, Tom. Find Merlin, but be safe. And tell Arthur and Woodsmoke not to worry." She turned back to Nimue. "Tell me what you want me to do."

Half an hour later, Tom, Woodsmoke and Arthur were on Raghnall's path heading higher on the mountain. It had been difficult for Tom to persuade them to leave, but finally they had set off.

"Are you sure they want to stay, Tom?" Woodsmoke had asked, puzzled. "I don't trust Nimue."

"Well they do. And she needs them. And we need Nimue, so …" He'd shrugged.

Arthur had headed into the house, but Tom had stopped him at the back door, shouting, "Arthur, do you want to find Merlin or not? We can't do both."

Arthur had returned to his horse, saying, "I feel I'm abandoning them."

"They're all very capable Arthur," Woodsmoke said. "We have to respect their decision."

"If anything happens to them ..." Arthur began.

"Then we'll all be to blame," Tom answered. "How was Magen?"

"Furious. But he thought better of arguing and went up on the city walls with the rest of his guards. I'm not sure I'll be welcomed back to the city, but–" Arthur shrugged and sighed. "We'd better go."

They'd headed up the path behind Raghnall's house and found that Woodsmoke was right. The landslide had disappeared and the way was clear. But it was now pitch black and the path ahead was almost invisible.

Arthur dismounted. "I'll lead. We'll take it slowly."

"Arthur, this seems like suicide," Tom said, as loose rock slipped beneath his feet and he tried to steady himself against Midnight. It was surprising how much he'd got used to his horse, he thought, as he struggled up the hill. She'd become a reassuring presence.

"Just keep going, Tom," Woodsmoke said from behind him. "I can't see Raghnall risking his life on a poorly made path, it must be pretty safe."

"In the light, maybe," Tom muttered.

After a short while they crested a ridge and looked back to see the city, and the House of the Beloved, below them in the hollow of the mountain. Magen must have warned the fey of imminent attack – either that or they had seen the dragons, because half the city was now in darkness and they could just make out the faint glow of the braziers on the roof of Raghnall's house. The city walls were well lit with torches, and the firelight glinted on the crossbows that sat atop the wall.

Suddenly, one of the dragons dived straight at the city, but before it could get close a flurry of huge arrows was released and the dragon withdrew with a roar, belching flames onto the roof of one of the highest buildings. It immediately burst into flames which, within seconds, were reaching high into the night sky.

"The city's burning!" Tom exclaimed.

"Not yet, Tom," Woodsmoke said, trying to reassure him. "I'm sure they must have plans for this."

"I knew we shouldn't have left," Arthur grumbled.

"But we couldn't have stopped this," Woodsmoke said. "Come on, we have to get as far as we can by daybreak. At least the dragons will be preoccupied. Too preoccupied to hear your sword, I hope, Arthur, because now Raghnall's dead the spell he put on the scabbard is gone."

A skittering of rocks caused them to spin away from the city back towards the high pass.

"What was that?" Tom asked, his right hand moving to Galatine.

They stood listening for a few seconds, but heard nothing else.

"Just rock fall," Arthur said. "Certainly not a dragon."

They moved slowly over the rock-strewn ground, lit faintly by a half moon above them. The path here was easier to follow and they picked up their pace, all the time moving higher and higher up the mountain, until the path met another and they found themselves on the broad main pass. They heaved a sigh of relief, but it was short lived. Something reared up beneath Farlight, and Woodsmoke fell from his horse, crashing to the ground. Within seconds a large writhing serpent was upon him, and with a scream of terror, Farlight raced away.

Tom and Arthur dropped to the ground, weapons drawn, and ran across to Woodsmoke, only then realising that the snake had the head and body of a woman. It was the lamia that Bloodmoon had been tracking. She snapped and bit at Woodsmoke's face, trying to sink her long teeth into his neck, her hands pushing his shoulders against the ground. His left arm was pinned against his body, but with his right hand he pushed her head back, keeping it inches from his own. Her strong muscular body continued to wrap tightly around his chest, and Woodsmoke struggled for breath as her teeth inched nearer and nearer.

Scared of using their swords in case they stabbed Woodsmoke, Arthur and Tom used their combined strength to pull the serpent off him, throwing her across the ground. She reared up and lunged at Arthur. He swung Excalibur, but she reared back before striking again.

Woodsmoke struggled to his feet, clutching his ribs, as Tom and Arthur advanced on the lamia. Her tail flicked out beneath Tom's feet and he stumbled backwards, rolling to his feet again. She was frighteningly quick, and she leapt on Arthur, wrapping her tail around his legs and pinning him to the ground.

Just as Tom was thinking he could never pull her from Arthur on his own, another figure ran to his side. Bloodmoon. "Tom!" he yelled. "Pull her head back. Just grab her hair."

Tom got as close as he could, stepping across Arthur's and the lamia's prone bodies, and grabbed a handful of her hair, pulling her head up with all his strength.

"Arthur, keep your head down!" Bloodmoon yelled, and he stood behind Arthur, his sword ready to strike. "Tom, pull higher!"

The lamia was incredibly strong, but as she realised what was happening she loosened her grip on Arthur, allowing Tom to pull her head high above Arthur's chest. Without hesitating, Bloodmoon attacked, his sword passing within inches of Tom's chest, swiping her head off and leaving it swinging from Tom's hands. Hot blood spat from her neck, and her body slumped across Arthur's, convulsing in its death throes.

Tom yelled in horror and threw her head away, watching it roll across the ground, the jaw wide and the long teeth glinting.

"Can somebody get this thing off me?" Arthur groaned, and he pushed against the lamia's body. Bloodmoon and Tom pulled the still-twitching body off Arthur and then stood trying to catch their breath.

Bloodmoon grinned at Tom. "I timed that well!"

"You call that good timing? Five minutes earlier would have been better."

"Not as much fun, though," Bloodmoon said, striding over and picking up the lamia's head. He examined it in the moonlight, saying, "I lost her earlier, but only briefly. She's been very tricky."

"So now you can claim your reward, cousin," Woodsmoke said. "You should give us a share. I think she's broken my ribs."

Bloodmoon laughed. "Good try, but I don't think so." He strode across to his pack and, pulling a large sack free, lowered the lamia's head into it. "I'll take this with me for proof. And now I think it's time for a drink." He took a large bottle from his bag, pulled the cork out with his teeth and drank deeply. "Anyone else?"

Three hands shot out as, in unison, they said, "Yes please."

Chapter 27 The House of Smoke and Glass

They reached the pass into the Sky Meadows at dawn. It was an unassuming break in the rock, and on the other side an expanse of fields stretched ahead of them, encompassed by a ring of rock. Drifts of mist rose from the ground, mingling with the scent of wild flowers and grass.

High above them was a city in the air, its buildings shimmering in the pale dawn light, and in the centre of the meadows was a beam of light leading to the city above. The sound of water drew them to their left, and they found a stream running into a shallow pool.

"Thank the gods," Arthur said, as they dismounted. "I stink of lamia blood."

"Is it worse than dragon blood?" Woodsmoke asked.

"Actually I think it is. There's more of it on me, anyway." And he was right. The entire front of his body was covered in blood that was now drying in thick crusty clots. It was even in his hair.

Tom glanced down at his shirt where a broad splatter of blood from the lamia's beheading had landed across his chest. "The sylphs will wonder what's going on if we turn up like this. Honestly, Arthur. Two beheadings in one day." He tried to push the memory of killing the servant to the back of his mind.

"I am not responsible for the second one!" Arthur exclaimed.

"Three beheadings in a week!" Woodsmoke reminded them. "You *are* responsible for the dragon, though, Arthur."

Throwing off their clothes they waded into the pool, washing away the blood and dust.

"Does anyone need to rest?" Arthur asked.

Woodsmoke winced as he explored his bruised ribs. "No, let's just get on with it. But I should warn you, if the sylphs choose to attack, we will have no chance."

"Why not?" Tom asked.

"They're a warrior race, much stronger than we are, and our weapons will be of little use against them. Even Excalibur. There's a reason the other realms let them be."

With Woodsmoke's warning ringing in their ears, they tied the horses up next to the pool and set off on foot, striding through the waist-high grasses. It reminded Tom of the meadows outside Finnlugh's Under-Palace.

The Sky Meadows seemed eerily devoid of life. There were no other fey or sylphs, and they crossed in silence. Soon they reached the beam of light which, close up, was much larger than Tom expected.

"What are we supposed to do now?" he asked.

"There's only one way to find out," Arthur said, and stepped into it.

"Arthur, wait," Woodsmoke said, reaching to grab his arm.

But he'd gone, disappearing in a split second.

Tom looked around, alarmed. "Where's he gone?"

Woodsmoke sighed. "Up there, I hope. Come on, let's follow, and hope it's not going to kill us."

They stepped through together, and instantly Tom felt a sensation similar to that he'd experienced in the portals, although it was over more quickly. The feeling had barely registered before he found himself on a large platform facing a walled city. Arthur and Woodsmoke stood next to him.

Tom looked down and let out an involuntary yelp. "I can see through the floor!"

Far below were the Sky Meadows, a small patch of green amongst the mountain ridges. He clutched his stomach. "I feel sick. Is the floor safe?" he asked, tentatively stretching out a toe.

Woodsmoke took a few paces and looked back at Tom, grinning. "I think we're good, Tom."

"So this is the Realm of Air," Arthur said, looking impressed.

The city was a white-walled vision. It stretched ahead of them, the curve of its walls disappearing into drifting clouds at either side. But more impressive was its height. A multitude of buildings soared high above them, disappearing into the clouds. Every now and then the clouds drifted away, and Tom could see towers glittering in rays of sunshine.

They headed to the city gates and were met by a sylph carrying a long silver spear. He was far taller than them, and his body-length wings were tucked behind him. Unnervingly he was dressed for combat, wearing a breastplate and armguards, and he had the hardened face of the battle-ready. He was pale and blonde, and Tom felt he was in the presence of an angel.

"Welcome to the Realm of Air. What do you seek here?"

"We seek Merlin," Arthur said. "We believe he was brought here."

"And you are?"

Arthur introduced them all. "We were with him at Ceridwen's Cauldron."

The sylph looked at them thoughtfully. "Yes, we who guard the city have been warned to expect you."

"Warned?" Arthur asked cautiously. "We are his friends. We helped resurrect him. Can you take us to him?"

"No. You are to go to Adalyn, Commander of the City Guard. She wishes to see you first. Follow me."

He led them up a series of stairs built into the walls, until finally they emerged into a circular tower looking out across the city. The broad windows were open and a chill breeze drifted into the room. Seated at a central table was an older white-haired sylph. She lifted her head from the papers in front of her as they entered, and Tom was shocked to see a large scar that began on her right cheek and continued across where her right eye should have been. It was rare to see disfigurement in the fey.

"Adalyn. Merlin's companions from the Cauldron are here."

She sighed. "You have come. We weren't sure you would." She turned to the sylph. "You may go."

"Why wouldn't I?" Arthur asked, bristling with annoyance as the door shut behind them. "My reunion with Merlin was interrupted. I thought I'd try again."

She stood up, towering over all of them. "I do not apologise for rescuing Merlin when he summoned us. He felt vulnerable with the witch Nimue in your company."

"Nimue was not with us," Arthur retorted angrily.

Adalyn held her hand up to stop Arthur. "I do not accuse you of betraying him," she said softly. "All those who are twice born feel weak on awakening. Her presence was an unpleasant reminder of his imprisonment."

Tom took a deep breath of relief as the tension in the room seemed to dissipate, and sensed Arthur also taking a moment to gather himself.

"So, we can see him?" he continued. "We have travelled a long way."

"What is your intent?" she asked, moving around the table.

"Just to see him. I want to make sure he is all right, and then we leave. That's all."

"You are?"

"Arthur, King of the Britons. Merlin's very old friend," he added, a little defiantly.

"Yes, of course." She smiled, looking far less severe. "He has talked of you recently. Where is the witch now?"

They shuffled nervously as Arthur answered, "In Dragons' Hollow, defending the city and rebuilding the spell."

Adalyn looked confused. "Why does she need to rebuild the spell?"

Crap. Tom glanced at the other two, who like him were trying to look as innocent as possible.

"Because Raghnall has died, and therefore the spell has ceased to work," Arthur said vaguely.

Arthur looked the most uncomfortable Tom had ever seen him, and they must all be wondering the same things. How well did the sylphs get on with Raghnall? Would they be upset at his death? And how much trouble would they be in if they knew Arthur had killed him?

But all Adalyn said was, "So the passage to the Sky Meadows may close again." She shrugged. "It does not concern us. I shall escort you to Merlin's house."

As they followed her to the top of the city walls, where the winds were strong and cold, Tom sensed her shrug of indifference was not quite what it seemed.

Adalyn pointed to where towers pinnacled into the sky and the sylphs flew, their wings catching the light. "Merlin's house is on the edge of the city, where there are roads. For those without wings, the inner city is impossible to access."

She was right, Tom noted uneasily, he couldn't see a single road or staircase.

Adalyn led them down the length of the wall to where a bridge, which seemed to made of gossamer-thin glass, spanned the drop below. Crossing it, they came to a tower of smoky white glass. She led them up another spiral staircase until they reached an arched doorway.

"I'll leave you here," she said. "I presume you can make your own way back." Without waiting for an answer, she went over to an archway in the wall and stepped out, expanding her wings as she dropped, before soaring not to the city walls, Tom noticed, but over them to the Sky Meadows below.

Arthur was already knocking on the door, but Tom looked at Woodsmoke. "Did you see that?"

"No, what?"

"She flew down to the Sky Meadows. I think we're in trouble."

Before he could explain further, the door flew open and an irate Merlin stood before them. "Why are you disturbing me?" He fell silent as he registered who they were, and then said in shock, "Arthur, I didn't think you'd come." He stepped forward and grabbed him tightly.

Merlin ushered them into his room, and Tom immediately noticed its resemblance to the tower in the spell. It was full of tables and books, rocks, herbs, and gemstones, and on the far side was a large messy bed. But this room was much bigger, and its walls and ceiling were made of smoky glass that dimmed the dazzling light from outside, casting strange shadows in the room.

Merlin was as Tom remembered him. His hair was long, grey and tangled, and his beard grew thick and strong, halfway down his chest. But now his expression was full of life and vigour, and he seemed none the worse for his long imprisonment and death.

He looked at Tom and Woodsmoke, his face creasing into wrinkles as he smiled. "And who are these?"

"Woodsmoke is a good friend from the Realm of Earth," Arthur said, squeezing Woodsmoke's shoulder. Woodsmoke nodded and shook Merlin's hand, and Tom felt relieved that his anger with Arthur seemed long forgotten.

Then Arthur turned to Tom. "And Tom is a long-distance descendant of mine. He woke me from my long sleep. I'm sure you remember that bargain, Merlin?"

Merlin's piercing blue eyes fixed on Tom like a bird of prey. "Of course I remember."

Tom almost stuttered as he said hello.

"It seems Tom has a knack for breaking long sleeps," Arthur added. "He helped break Nimue's spell, too."

"I really didn't," Tom repeated, for what felt like the millionth time. "Herne broke the spell, not me."

"But you helped! The shaman said so," Arthur insisted.

"Herne was involved? How?" Merlin asked.

"The Cervini summoned him."

"Herne," Merlin repeated, "and the Cervini. Names I have not heard in a long time. The Cervini were there when Nimue's spell was broken?"

Arthur nodded. For a few seconds, Merlin was lost in thought, then he turned to Tom. "How did you help?"

"I used your spell books, actually." He shrugged. "I was desperate."

"And Vivian still lives? She summoned you here to wake Arthur?"

"Sort of, in a very indirect way," Tom said, trying not to say something mean about Vivian.

Merlin took a deep breath as if steeling himself for bad news. "And Nimue, where is she now?"

"In Dragon's Hollow. She will not harm you further, Merlin," Arthur reassured him.

"I do not fear Nimue – except for those few seconds when I awoke. I was so confused," he said. "So much noise, so much light. It was too much. I cast the first spell I could think of to take me to the securest place I knew." He gestured around him. "As for Nimue, everything she did, I let her do. Even while I was teaching her the spell, I knew she would turn it against me. I almost welcomed it." His eyes lost their intensity for a moment as he stared back into the past.

"Do you remember it all? The imprisonment, I mean?" Tom asked.

"It was like a beautiful dream," Merlin said softly.

"Come," Arthur insisted, "I want to hear about everything that's happened."

They sat before the fireplace, and while they talked Tom drifted over to the smoked glass walls, peering through to the city beyond. Of all the places he'd been so far, this felt the most alien. The sylphs were very different to the other fey, both in appearance and demeanour. Their appearance at the Cauldron had been swift, aggressive and unnerving, and they had seemed so pale they shimmered. Now he was here he had a feeling they shouldn't have come.

Woodsmoke joined him. "Why do you think we're in trouble, Tom?"

"Arthur killed Raghnall," Tom said quietly. "What if this breaks some sort of deal they had with him? You said it yourself, they are a warrior race. Warriors need weapons. What better place to get them than from the Hollow?"

Woodsmoke looked thoughtful. "Didn't Raghnall say the meeting he was going to was something to do with trade agreements with the sylphs? Trade with them would be very lucrative, even if the sylphs got their weapons for better prices than everyone else."

"If the city falls, the sylphs' main source of weapons will be gone," Tom said, his worry doubling. "They'll be very angry."

"But now Nimue is the key to protecting the city, and Arthur is surely protected by Merlin."

They talked quietly for a while, discussing the possibilities, and then Merlin called them over. "Come, you must join us."

Merlin had placed food and drink on the table in front of the fire, and Tom realised he hadn't eaten for hours.

"If you're sure we aren't interrupting you," Tom said, lowering himself into a chair and reaching for a glass.

They talked for hours, Merlin asking them all sorts of questions about the other realms and the other Earth. It was obvious that Arthur and Merlin had real affection for each other, and for a time, Tom's worry disappeared. They were finally interrupted when long shadows flashed across the room, and the door flew open.

Adalyn stepped into the room with three sylphs behind her, and glared at Arthur, Tom and Woodsmoke.

Merlin stood. "What's going on, Adalyn?"

"Arthur and Woodsmoke, you are under arrest for the murder of Raghnall, Sorcerer of Dragon's Hollow. Tom, you are arrested for the death of Grindan, Raghnall's servant."

Tom and Woodsmoke sat momentarily stunned, while Arthur leapt to his feet and unsheathed Excalibur. But Merlin stepped in front of him, his face thunderous. "How dare you arrest Arthur! And here, in my home!"

Adalyn advanced, her face rigid with anger. "Raghnall is dead, Merlin. Killed by Arthur."

Arthur squared up to her. "Because he was trying to kill all of us! For this," he said, brandishing Excalibur. "Do you think I would stand there and let him?"

Adalyn briefly looked at Excalibur, then said icily, "And Nimue stands in his place to protect the city! It seems you have divided loyalties, Arthur. She is currently under guard while she completes the spell, and then she will come here to answer to us. In the meantime you will be locked away until the trial."

Chapter 28 Tower of Winds

"You are making a mistake Adalyn. You don't need to lock them up, let them stay here while you investigate," Merlin said.

"So that you can engineer their escape? I don't think so."

"Then don't make it worse by using the tower in the city. I would like to visit them; they are entitled to support. Or are you so eager for a conviction that you don't respect your own laws any more?" he said scornfully.

"How quickly you insult us, Merlin," Adalyn sneered. "Do not presume too much on our hospitality. Whilst some are happy to have you returned to us, there are others for whom you are only a memory and a story. Since then many new alliances have been forged which surpass your importance to the Realm of Air."

"See it as a request from an old man who pleads for his friends," he said, clearly trying to control his temper. "If I can remind you, I am here because they rescued me. That deserves some leniency, surely. I think Galen would see it that way."

She narrowed her eyes at the mention of that name. "Use the Tower of Winds," she said to those behind her.

"And I will speak to the city elders." Merlin turned to Arthur. "Trust me, Arthur, I will get you out of this. Have patience." He pressed Arthur's hand.

Woodsmoke nodded in agreement, and Arthur reluctantly sheathed Excalibur. Woodsmoke then said quietly to Tom, "This is not the time to pick a fight, Tom. Our chance will come."

They were unceremoniously escorted to a high tower at a place far along the city walls, and an hour later they sat looking out over clouds. Their prison was a series of small rooms with hard beds, plain chairs and a central room with one big table. On their way to the top floor they had passed at least five other levels with secure doors, but all the doors stood wide, and the prison tower was clearly empty except for them.

Tom was relieved they weren't locked up in separate rooms, and as the door slammed shut behind them, they stared bleakly at each other.

"What now?" Tom asked.

"We wait," Arthur said. "We'll see what Merlin can do, but if he doesn't succeed …" he shrugged, "we may have to fight our way out."

Woodsmoke stood by the window, surveying their surroundings. There weren't any bars, and the windows could open, which wasn't really surprising. Where would they go? "I wonder if Brenna and Beansprout will be arrested."

"They haven't done anything. I'm more worried about Nimue and what she may do," Arthur said.

Tom remembered his conversation with Nimue in the spell. "She said she always liked to be underestimated. I think that will work in our favour."

Arthur nodded. "She's resourceful, I'll give her that. She always surprised me — and not always in a good way."

They passed the next few hours playing cards, but none of them were really paying attention. Night was falling when they were disturbed by a large black bird rapping its beak on the windows.

Woodsmoke grinned. "Brenna!" He let her in and she flew in and changed form, scanning the room.

"So you couldn't go five minutes without getting into trouble!" she said, exasperated.

Arthur looked sheepish. "We didn't do anything! Except kill Raghnall and his servant. I must admit I didn't consider this might happen."

"It took some time to track you down. I checked out the highest, most-isolated towers. There's a lot of them."

"What's happening in Dragon's Hollow?" Woodsmoke asked. "Has Nimue worked the spell?"

"Not quite. The sylphs' arrival has delayed things. As soon as they arrived, I knew we were in trouble. They searched the house and interrogated us. I thought they were going to arrest all of us," she said, looking tired and frustrated. "We tried to explain what had happened but they didn't want explanations. They were going to arrest Nimue as soon as they arrived, but then realised that would be incredibly stupid. They were attacked by dragons as they flew in."

"Is the city burning?" Tom asked. "We saw the dragon attack from the ridge."

"A couple of buildings were partially destroyed, but some of the fey have magic strong enough to slow fire." She sighed. "But they keep attacking. Only the dragon guard and the crossbows are slowing them down. They're ripping away all the gold and jewels from the highest buildings. And with each success they grow bolder."

"Is Beansprout all right?" Arthur asked. "Have they threatened to arrest her?"

"No, they haven't – or me. She's helping Nimue, and is doing very well. She seems quite interested in magic."

Tom wondered whether to say anything about their previous argument, but decided not to. Beansprout might be right about Nimue. He did think of something else though. "Do you think Nimue might resist arrest, like she did with the Cervini?"

"Oh no. In fact she's looking forward to coming here. I think she has a plan."

Brenna stayed with them a while longer before swooping back to the Hollow, promising to return with more news.

Their next visitor was Merlin, who arrived breathless and grumpy.

"Galen is not as sympathetic as I thought. He insists you be tried before the high court. All of you."

"Who is this Galen?" Arthur asked.

"A very old friend. One of the few who was alive in my time. He sits at the head of the Council of Judgement. There are six of them, and the others are younger. They don't know me at all. Galen is under pressure to serve justice. There aren't any kings, queens, princes or princesses here. The Council rules on everything and their power is absolute."

"What could the consequences be?" Woodsmoke asked, his usual relaxed demeanour replaced with an alert watchfulness.

"A guilty charge could be anything from banishment or imprisonment to death."

"Death?" Tom said, alarmed. "Don't we get a lawyer or something?" he asked, thinking of how justice worked at home.

"I have no idea what one of those is, Tom," Merlin said, "so no. Friends may plead on your behalf, but that's all.

However," he added, in an effort to reassure them, "I am one of the most powerful wizards ever, and I am pleased to say that after my long period of imprisonment my powers remain as strong as ever. That said, I cannot take on the entire Realm of Air. Therefore, if things go badly in court, I will ensure you get away, but you'd be fugitives. Forever. We must resolve this legally, with no repercussions."

"When will we be seen?" Arthur asked. He looked pale, but his voice held a steely determination.

"The day after tomorrow, at dawn, at the Palace of Reckoning, in front of the seven who sit on the Reckoning Panel."

"So soon!" Tom said, not sure if this was a good thing or not.

"The issue is not just about you, it's also about the spell and the repercussions. They want to settle this quickly. It's a public trial, so others will be there." He paused and sighed softly. "I must confess, I think my long imprisonment has addled my brain a little." Merlin rested his gaze on Arthur. "I had almost forgotten about the dragon wars, it was so long ago."

"The dragon wars?" Tom asked, thinking that sounded utterly terrifying.

Woodsmoke nodded. "That was a long time ago, even in our long lifetimes."

"For years," Merlin explained, "the Realm of Air waged an intermittent, long and bloody war with the dragons. At first, Dragon Skin Mountain was home to only a handful of dragons. Most of them lived in the deserts of the Djinn – the Realm of Fire. But as the Djinn claimed more land, the dragons came here, drawn to the rich reserves of the mountain, and they ravaged the lands and attacked the sylphs.

Until Raghnall came along to contain them. His spell allowed access to the dragon gold, the small village grew into the city it is now, and he gave peace to the sylphs. Raghnall's death has far-reaching consequences."

"Raghnall must have been really old!" Tom said, trying to work it out.

"Very old. I met him once, briefly. I never liked him so avoided him after that."

"And his spell extended here?" Tom tried to get his head around the size of the spell Raghnall had made.

"The dragons could attack again; the sylphs would be at war," Arthur said, as understanding dawned.

"Adalyn was right. I have no influence here. Not any more. I am a man out of my time." Suddenly Merlin's defiance crumbled, and his shoulders sagged as he looked into some indeterminate future. "Maybe you shouldn't have woken me. I realise now this is not my home, and whatever happens I cannot continue to live here." He looked at Arthur in panic. "Where will I go?"

Merlin's hands were clutched together on the table, and Arthur reached forward, resting his hand on Merlin's. "We will get out of here, and you will live with me, close to the Cervini. You do have friends here Merlin, as do I," Arthur said, smiling at the others. "I am also a man out of time, but we will walk new paths, old friend."

Merlin gave Arthur's hand a squeeze and smiled at him with affection. "I hope you are right." Gathering his courage, he stood and nodded to them all. "I will see you tomorrow with any news." He swept from the room, his worn grey cloak swinging behind him.

The reality of their situation was now clear to Tom, and he felt a horrible tightness in the pit of his stomach. He hadn't decided to live here only to be on the run. But he had killed someone, he thought, feeling sick at the memory. And then, with a sudden pang, he thought of his granddad. He hadn't seen him for weeks. What if he never saw him again? He had no idea of where they were or what was happening. And Fahey and Finnlugh? Tom had taken it for granted he'd see them all again, but now he might never be able to. Perhaps he'd never see Beansprout again!

He tried to be positive. "They aren't going to kill us. I think the worst that might happen is banishment. And I really don't ever want to come here again anyway."

"Maybe," Woodsmoke said, leaning back into his chair, his long legs resting on the table top. "But I'm not sure I share your confidence. I hate feeling we're relying on Nimue."

Tom slept badly. Only the fact that he'd been up for more than twenty-four hours meant he slept at all. The bed was hard and lumpy, the blankets too thin, and his mind raced with horrible possibilities. It was only with the dawn that he managed to sleep deeply for a few hours.

He was woken by voices in the main room, and he blearily stumbled through to find Brenna was back. She looked up as Tom entered and gave him a faint smile. "Nimue is here, in another tower. Her trial's the same time as yours."

"How do you know?" Arthur asked, looking as if he'd had a bad night's sleep too. His hair was uncombed and his clothes were dishevelled.

She looked grim. "I eavesdropped with great difficulty. Anyway, the spell is complete, sort of, and the city is safe, but very damaged."

"But how long will the spell last if she's here?" Tom asked, worried about Beansprout.

"Long enough. Nimue has plans, I'm not sure what. She's very good at secrets. I'd better get back to check on Beansprout. If I can't return, good luck for tomorrow." Brenna wasn't normally affectionate, but she was now, and she hugged all of them. "One way or another, we'll get you out of here."

After Brenna left, they spent the day pacing around the narrow confines of the tower rooms. Merlin visited, looking drawn and anxious, bringing news that a representative from Dragon's Hollow was going to be at the trial as well. It was a long, horrible day of waiting.

Chapter 29   Excalibur's Song

On the morning of the trial they were woken early, while the sky was still dark. A heavily armed sylph with eyes so pale as to be almost colourless, entered with a tray of food, which he left on the table.

Tom felt shattered. He had barely slept with worry, and the sound of the wind blowing relentlessly around the tower intruded into his dreams. He forced down some food in an effort to fortify himself for the trial.

They were all quiet, locked within their own thoughts. Half an hour later the sylph returned with another, and they were escorted down the long winding stairs.

Outside on the broad walls, the freezing wind sliced through Tom's cloak, and he started shivering. Half a dozen sylphs surrounded a large metal basket into which they were hustled, its door firmly locked behind them.

The sylphs then took hold of short chains attached to the top and sides, and they were lifted into the air and carried across the city towards the Palace of Reckoning. Tom had never been so cold in his life. Or so scared. Or so breathless, he realised, as he struggled to get a full lungful of air – they were incredibly high. Below them, the city was beautiful, in a stark and unforgiving way. In the dawn pallor it was all shades of grey, with pockets of blackness imposed by hard angles and high towers. Flashes of gold and silver decorated the walls and the tips of towers, the glinting metals making the place seem even colder. He hugged his cloak around him and thought longingly of Dragon's Hollow, the House of the Beloved, and the bed he'd slept in there.

The sun was just emerging over the far horizon when the palace came into view. Tom caught a glimpse of a broad terrace along one side, before they were lowered into the palace courtyard. Nothing here was small, Tom thought, feeling insignificant as he gazed up at the walls, their lofty heights disappearing into the grey haze of dawn.

When the cage door was unlocked, Tom, Arthur and Woodsmoke walked around the shadowy courtyard, stamping vigorously to keep warm. The sylphs watched them, clearly impervious to the cold.

Nimue arrived alone, in a smaller cage, escorted by two sylphs. She looked tiny and defenceless, barely half the height of the sylphs towering over her, but she moved with a steady, almost stately grace, as the sylphs ushered her to the far side of the courtyard. Clearly she was being kept apart from Tom and the others before the trial. She glanced over at them, giving a barely perceptible smile and nod, before turning away.

Within minutes, Merlin arrived in another single cage. Tom glanced anxiously at Nimue, but she ignored him, deep in thought.

Merlin didn't waste time on greetings. "The terrace is almost full already."

"Full of what?" Tom asked, distracted by Nimue in the distance.

Merlin looked at him impatiently. "Sylphs! Come to watch your trial!"

"Oh, of course," Tom said, embarrassed.

Woodsmoke gave him a sidelong look full of amusement. "Keep your mind on the moment, Tom," he said softly.

"Bringing you here means they want to make an example of you," Merlin continued, his face full of worry. "There are smaller places where they hold trials, but none of them has the pomp of this place." He looked around distastefully.

They were interrupted by an ancient sylph, his face creased with age, his wings a dark grizzled grey.

"Galen," Merlin said. "Are you sure you want to do this?"

"Justice must be served," the sylph muttered angrily. He glared at the three of them, his gaze finally settling on Arthur. "Arthur, I presume?"

Arthur nodded and tried to shake his hand, but Galen ignored him, saying only, "You will be tried first," before stalking off into the palace.

"I have a feeling this morning is not going to go well," Arthur said.

The terrace was a windswept place stretching away from the palace. Immediately beyond the main building was a row of pillars supporting a deep roofed walkway. Four seats had been placed in front of the pillared walk, and Tom and the others stood before them, gazing out at the crowd gathered in tiered seats that rose like an amphitheatre.

The sylphs were silent. There were no hushed conversations or debates; instead they sat like statues. Even more unnerving was the row of women-headed bird creatures perched along the highest row of the terrace. Even at a distance he could see their beady eyes and sharp teeth.

He whispered, "Woodsmoke, what are they?"

"Harpies, the constant companions of the sylphs," Woodsmoke said. "They'll steal food from your plate and leave you to starve to death. And then feed on your body."

Tom wished he hadn't asked.

Between them and the crowd was a long stone table with seven sylphs seated behind it, facing them, their backs to the audience. They were a range of ages, with different wings, from white, to tawny greys, dark browns and silvers – but they all looked serious. In the centre was Galen. Seated to the side was one of the fey from Dragon's Hollow.

Tom turned to his right and looked at Nimue, who was now standing next to him. Feeling his gaze upon her, she gave him the ghost of a smile before turning back to the crowd.

Galen stood, and his voice boomed across the space as if he had a microphone. "The four who stand before us are all accused of murder. The repercussions of their actions will impact on the safety of this realm, and their punishment will fit their crimes accordingly. Arthur, once King of Britain, will be tried first. Woodsmoke, Tom and Nimue, you may sit until called."

Tom sat pondering Galen's description of Arthur as "Once King of Britain." It was as if he wanted to remind them that Arthur wasn't powerful any more. He looked at Arthur, who stood rigid, facing Galen and the others. Tom had no idea what he might be feeling.

None of them had been allowed their weapons. Arthur's reclaimed weapons and armour sat on the table in front of the panel, along with Excalibur, Galatine, Woodsmoke's bow, sword, and hunting knife, and Brionac.

"Arthur," Galen began, "you face the most serious charge of all, as you instigated the attack on Raghnall. We found his head lying in the weapons room of the House of the Beloved. His body lay outside the room, a deep wound in the chest made from this spear here," he gestured to Brionac, "which we know to have been thrown by Woodsmoke, a fey of the Realm of Earth. Do you admit your guilt?"

"Yes, I do," Arthur said, his voice also booming out across the terrace. "But as he was trying to kill my friends and me, I feel justified." His voice held no trace of regret.

"We have no evidence of his attack on you," Galen said stiffly, "only the wounds of two weapons suggesting an unequal attack."

Woodsmoke stood and shouted, "You have the word of the three people sitting here with Arthur!"

Galen glared at him. "Sit down! You are all conspirators. Of course you will support each other."

"You have evidence to the contrary? That he wasn't attacking Arthur?" Nimue asked. Unlike Woodsmoke, she remained seated, her hands resting in her lap.

"No! And I do not need any. We of the Panel of Reckoning know Raghnall. He would not attempt to kill anyone. Sit down!"

The city guards grabbed Woodsmoke across the shoulders and forced him to sit. Tom felt sick. This was not a trial. There was no evidence in their favour. Merlin was right. They were going to make an example of them.

Galen continued. "There are weapons here that have been taken from Raghnall's collection. So you are all thieves as well?"

"No. I claim what is mine," Arthur explained. "Many of those weapons were mine in my lifetime. Raghnall was the thief, he tried to take Excalibur. By force."

Galen picked up Excalibur. "This is Excalibur?"

"It is."

Galen drew Excalibur from its scabbard, and the rising sun glittered along its length, throwing beams of light across the terrace. Tom glanced again at Nimue, and although she didn't look at him, she smiled her shy soft smile again.

"It is fine workmanship," Galen said admiringly.

"Made by the Forger of Light," Merlin said, from where he stood on the other side of Arthur.

A ripple of unease passed across the watching crowd, prompting some sign of life at last.

Galen looked up quickly and crashed Excalibur back onto the table. "Do not mention his name here!" he said furiously. Tom felt a stir of curiosity at what the Forger of Light had done. "That is irrelevant. Arthur, you have murdered Raghnall, and by doing so have placed us at risk of attack from dragons. Your sentence is death. At the end of these proceedings you shall be dropped from the terrace. The fall will be long enough for you to consider your actions."

Tom drew his breath in sharply and looked in horror at Galen and Arthur. Involuntarily he rose to feet, as Woodsmoke shouted, "No! It's not fair!"

Arthur didn't speak, but he glared at Galen defiantly before glancing around the terrace, and Tom realised he was assessing their chance of escape. Arthur wouldn't give up without a fight.

Galen sought to wrestle back control. "Tom, a human interloper in the affairs of the Realm of Air, and Woodsmoke, will also be put to death."

Tom felt faint. He could barely believe his ears.

"Woodsmoke, the spear you carried here is from Raghnall's weapons room and is the weapon that pierced Raghnall's chest. Do you deny it?"

Woodsmoke shook off the restraining hands of the sylphs and stood shoulder to shoulder with Arthur, and when he spoke his voice was as hard as steel. "No. I sought to protect my friends and would do it again."

"And Tom, you are responsible for the death of Grindan. The death of a harmless servant will not be tolerated."

"He was not harmless!" Tom exclaimed. "He tried to kill me! Look at the marks on my neck." And he pulled his cloak down, showing the bruising on his throat.

Galen refused to engage in conversation, instead looking at Nimue. "And so, we come to Nimue, the witch."

Merlin stepped forward, shouting, "Galen, they all helped to rescue me and are responsible for my resurrection. I beg you to take that into consideration."

"We have, Merlin. And while their actions to rescue you were admirable, their other actions far outweigh them. The sentence remains." Galen's tone was firm, and he turned away from Merlin and back to Nimue.

Tom felt as if the air had been ripped from his lungs and the bones ripped from his legs. He collapsed onto his chair and looked at Woodsmoke, but Woodsmoke was glaring at Galen, his fists clenched, unable to offer Tom any reassurance. Beyond him, Arthur was stony faced.

How could they hope to escape? They really were going to die.

"Nimue, please stand before the panel."

Nimue rose slowly to her feet, brushing off her gown as she stood, the only one who now looked composed.

"Your crime is that of imprisoning Merlin, lifelong friend of the Realm of Air, resulting in his eventual death. On his resurrection you then attempted to injure him once again, and were stopped only by our arrival."

Merlin again intervened. "I do not wish you to try Nimue. It is not your business."

"I decide what is tried here, Merlin, not you," Galen said. "Nimue, have you anything to say?"

She shrugged. "I have much to say on these charges, Galen, but what would be the point?"

Galen didn't seem to appreciate her tone, but continued. "Your casting of the spell of protection over Dragon's Hollow and the Realm of Air following Raghnall's death is much appreciated, and we will therefore commute your sentence from death to banishment from the Realm of Air, as long as you agree to maintain the spell in Dragon's Hollow."

"So you seek not to kill me, but to imprison me for life in the Hollow?" she asked, amused.

"You will keep your life." Galen glared at her.

"I am a witch of Avalon. Do you really think you could kill me or imprison me without magical help?" Her words fell into endless silence, and the panel twitched uncomfortably. Satisfied she had their full attention, she asked, "Who told you I have protected the Realm of Air?"

"Adalyn said you had finished the spell and extended protection to us." He looked to where Adalyn stood in the shadows of the pillared walkway.

"I have cast the spell to protect the city, but such was the speed of my arrest, I could not complete the circle of protection."

Adalyn stepped into the weak sunshine. "That is not true. We ascertained the spell has been completed."

Nimue sighed. "How careless of me. Was I not clear? What I should have said was that the spell to protect the Realm of Air had been completed, but was only temporary. It is now broken." She stood as if deep in thought. "In fact it probably finished at dawn. How long do you think it would take dragons to get here?"

As the full implications of her news sank in, she added, almost apologetically, "I did tell Adalyn that I really needed more time."

Adalyn glared at Nimue, but Tom felt a little bubble of hope starting to form inside him. And then there was a sound that chilled his blood – the far-off roar of dragons. Adalyn nodded to the guards standing behind them. All but two ran to the edge of the terrace and dived over, their wings spreading majestically before they dropped from sight. The other sylphs in the crowd rose restlessly, trying to see beyond the terrace, while the harpies cried out raucously for the blood of Tom, Woodsmoke and Arthur.

Galen looked furious. "I demand you complete the spell at once."

"I don't think so," Nimue said, her voice carrying clearly across the terrace, despite the increasing noise. "The Realm of Air can burn for all I care."

"You will complete the spell or we will bring your other friends here as well."

Her eyes bright were with malice. "No you won't. You'll find you cannot enter Dragon's Hollow at the moment. So what will you threaten to do now? You have already sentenced my friends to death."

"What do you mean, we cannot enter Dragon's Hollow?" Galen asked, incensed.

"I mean that once we left the city, I set a spell to prevent you entering it. Do you think I'm stupid?" Nimue asked, clearly enjoying herself.

Galen stood silent, the other sylphs sitting helplessly by his side as Adalyn strode over to Nimue and put the long blade of her sword to Nimue's throat. "Fix this now," Adalyn said, almost spitting in her face.

"No. If you kill me everything will fall. I'll tell you what I'm prepared to do. Please remove your sword."

Adalyn glanced at Galen, and at his nod reluctantly withdrew her sword.

Tom's heart pounded as he heard the dragons coming closer. The terraces were emptying as sylphs dived over the edge, spears extended, to join the fight.

"What?" yelled Galen, frustrated at Nimue's endless calm.

"You will release Arthur, Tom and Woodsmoke, and drop all charges against them. You will escort us from here to Dragon's Hollow. Or," she smirked, "as close as you can get. In exchange I will extend my protection to the Realm of Air."

She turned to the fey from the City Council. "I have decided I would like to stay in Dragon's Hollow. It will be my pleasure to live at the House of the Beloved and protect the city. If it pleases you?" she asked graciously. "Of course, I would like my friends to be able to visit me as often as they wish."

As Nimue finished speaking, a large red and black dragon soared up from below the terrace and released a stream of fire above their heads, before sylphs attacked it from all angles, drawing it out beyond the city. Tom watched as the bright white bodies of the sylphs turned and dived in the air, their spears flashing in the sun as the dragon whipped around, almost impervious to their attempts to wound it.

The fey paled and stuttered. "Y-You're welcome to live at Dragon's Hollow as long as you wish."

"Excellent. So, should we be going?" Nimue turned to smile at Adalyn. "Remember, I need to be in the Hollow to complete the spell."

Tom stood, stunned at the turn the morning had taken. Merlin gazed at Nimue, unable to hide the admiration and pride he felt, and Tom couldn't blame him. No wonder he'd been infatuated.

Adalyn looked to Galen for advice. He had fled from the table and now towered over Nimue, fury in his eyes and a dangerous tone to his voice. "You will never be welcome here again."

"Fortunately, I am far more understanding. I look forward to seeing you in Dragon's Hollow."

Galen turned to Tom, Woodsmoke and Arthur, glaring at each of them, and Tom had never felt more hated in his life. "Your sentences are reduced to banishment."

Tom felt his knees weaken with the relief of it all, but stood his ground next to Woodsmoke and Arthur, as if he'd never doubted the outcome in the first place.

Merlin interrupted. "I'm going with them, Galen. I really don't feel welcome here any more." He looked around at the view, and a shadow of regret crossed his face. "I'll send for my things later."

"As you wish," Galen said, making no attempt to dissuade him. To Adalyn he said, "Take them now."

As he finished speaking, more dragons burst into view, breathing long plumes of flames and pursued by sylphs. One, the colour of sulphurous yellow, flew low across the terrace, its claws extended, heading for the weapons on the table. Propelled into action, Tom, Arthur and Woodsmoke ran to grab their weapons, dodging and weaving amongst the flashing spears, flames and talons. Tom felt the searing heat of the flames pass over his head, and instinctively dropped and rolled. Regaining his feet, he grabbed Galatine and Arthur's shield before taking cover under the stone table. Looking out, all he could see were running feet and flames, and he heard roars as more dragons flew low over the terrace. Woodsmoke rolled next to him, preparing his bow, and Arthur joined him on his other side.

"I hope you're not planning to sit here all day?" Arthur shouted over the din.

"Of course not!" Tom said, wishing he could.

The thump of large clawed feet made them turn towards the far end of the table, where a dragon was trying his best to peer underneath. There was an enormous shudder as the heavy table started to move, and flames licked around them.

"Now!" shouted Woodsmoke, and before Tom could think they ran headlong towards the palace doors and temporary safety.

As Tom entered the broad echoing room behind the terrace, he almost collided with Nimue, who stood looking up at Merlin. They were both subdued, as if a full-scale battle wasn't going on outside at all.

"We could intervene now, drive back the dragons a little," Merlin said.

"No, they deserve this," Nimue replied, looking out with satisfaction on the results of her work. "I want them to remember this day, Merlin."

Chapter 30 Decisions and Deal Making

Nimue again subdued Excalibur's call, and half a dozen seething sylphs bundled them into the large cage and carried them down to the Sky Meadows.

The descent beneath the city was hazardous, and they were lucky the dragons were fully occupied high above them. Tom, Arthur and Merlin were deposited next to their horses, and with Merlin riding behind Arthur, they set off on the long ride back down the mountain. The sylphs took Nimue as far down the ridge as they were able so she arrived in the city quicker. From a distance she looked like a bird in a gilded cage.

Fortunately, they didn't encounter any dragons, and those they saw flew high overhead, as if drawn to the Realm of Air. Tom wondered if Nimue had cast some sort of spell that kept them attacking the sylphs. Every now and then he looked back to the city high above, and saw flashes of flame and glinting light and the swirl of sylphs. He tried to feel sorry for them, but couldn't. Even now, the thought of being sentenced to death seemed like a nightmare, and he kept wondering if, once the spell was resurrected, they would come back for him.

Woodsmoke tried to reassure him. "It's over, Tom. We have their word. And besides, Nimue would drop the spell like a thunderbolt if they ever threatened us again. They have too much to lose."

"What do you think about Nimue?" Tom asked, knowing Woodsmoke had been suspicious of her.

"There's a lot more to Nimue than meets the eye," he said, and then smiled at him. "I think she's too old for you, Tom!"

Tom felt himself blushing, and laughed. "I know! But I can look, can't I?"

"As long as that's all it is!" Woodsmoke said, teasing him. "I think she'd turn you into a toad if you tried anything."

The courtyard of Raghnall's House was dark when they arrived, the only light coming from a lantern that burned with a small golden flame over the door to the stables. Tom slipped off his horse, bone weary, his eyes struggling to stay open, but the sudden change of scene and the unsaddling of the horses woke him up again.

Merlin looked stiff as he dismounted. "So this is Raghnall's place?"

"Was," reminded Arthur. "I thought you'd met him."

"I did, but only in the city; I never came here." He looked around, his sharp eyes assessing everything. "He did quite well for himself, didn't he?"

"Wait till you see inside," Tom said, thinking longingly of his bed and hot bath.

Although they tried to be quiet, the clatter of hooves must have reached into the house, because it wasn't long before the back door flew open and Beansprout appeared, exclaiming, "Could you be any louder?"

"Thanks, Beansprout. Nice to see you too, after my brush with death," Tom said.

She strolled over to them, leaning on the open stable door. Her hair was loose, and she was wearing a long floaty dress he'd never seen before.

"What are you wearing?" Tom asked.

"It's called a dress, Tom. You know, not trousers."

"Ha, so funny. But why?"

"I think," Woodsmoke said, interrupting, "it's called the Nimue effect."

"Nice to see you too, Woodsmoke," she said, and poked out her tongue.

Arthur hugged her tightly. "I'm glad you're safe. You're becoming quite the warrior maiden."

She looked embarrassed. "Not really, Arthur! I just helped Nimue and Brenna."

"You stayed when you could have run," he told her. "That's very brave."

"Yes it is. A quality not to be underestimated," Merlin said, stepping out of the shadows, and rather than shake her extended hand, he kissed it. "My pleasure, my lady. Merlin, at your service."

"Beansprout, at yours," she said, her eyes sweeping over him. "I've come to show you to your room."

A look of concern crossed Merlin's face. "Are you sure I can stay here?"

"Of course. She told you so, didn't she?" Beansprout asked.

Tom recalled the brief conversation Nimue had had earlier with Merlin. It had been awkward. Nimue had been defiantly polite, as if she hadn't trapped him in a spell hundreds of years earlier, and Merlin had seemed almost meek and apologetic, as if he was responsible for everything in the first place.

"Well, yes," Merlin said hesitantly. "But I'm quite prepared to stay in a hotel."

"There's no need. She won't hear of it," Beansprout reassured him.

Arthur interrupted, frowning at Merlin. "Are you *sure* you want to stay here?"

"I am very tired, so just for tonight. I'll find somewhere else tomorrow. In the meantime," he said to Beansprout, "can I help to complete the spell to protect the Realm of Air?"

"It's done. Finally," Beansprout told them. Tom knew Beansprout wouldn't openly criticise Nimue, but she did look concerned. "Nimue didn't want to rush."

"She has a stubborn streak," Merlin said. "You'll get used to that."

The next morning, Tom woke to pale bands of sunshine streaking in round the edges of the heavy silk curtains. He was back in his old room, as he now thought of it.

Sitting up, he looked hopefully to where he'd left his clothes strewn across the floor, but they were still there, wrinkled and dirty. He flopped back on his pillows, huffing with disappointment. Then his stomach rumbled and he realised he was starving, so after dressing he made his way downstairs to the main balcony, where they had always eaten, but that too was empty. Wondering if he was completely alone, he shouted, "Hello? Anybody here?"

Silence.

Tom headed down the long corridor to the back of the house. This was where he'd been attacked. He was relieved to see the body of the servant had been removed, the place they'd fought marked only by a small patch of dried blood.

He carried on down to the cavernous kitchen, and that's where he found everyone. Arthur was standing over a flaming grill, cooking sausages, bacon and eggs, assisted by Merlin, who wore a long apron wrapped around his long flowing clothes. A slight odour of burning drifted around the room.

"Are you sure you know what you're doing?" Brenna asked, amused. She sat at a long wooden table, cradling a cup in her right hand, her chin on her left as she watched the activity across the room. Her long dark hair was bound at the nape of her neck, making the feathers that edged her hairline more obvious.

"Of course I do," Arthur said cheerily. "A little bit of burnt bacon makes it taste better."

Beansprout sat next to Nimue, and they were talking quietly. She gave Tom a guilty look as he sat down opposite them. Tom sensed a plan. "What's up, Beansprout?"

"Nothing," she said, wide-eyed with feigned surprise. "We're just discussing my future."

They gazed at him placidly across the table, and he felt his heart sink a little. "You're staying here, aren't you?"

After a second's hesitation, Beansprout nodded. "Nimue said she will teach me magic." She rushed on, "Don't look like that! Please be happy for me, Tom."

He sat not knowing what to say, and not even sure what he thought. He turned to Woodsmoke who had sat down next to him with a steaming cup of coffee. "What do you think?"

"I think Beansprout will be just fine," he said, looking at her a little sadly. "But we'll miss her at Vanishing Hall."

She met Woodsmoke's gaze and then looked quickly at the table, blinking back tears. "I won't be here forever, I'll come and visit."

"You'd better. What about you, Tom? Are you coming back with me?"

They were interrupted by Arthur and Merlin placing steaming plates of food in front of them.

"I thought you were coming with me to New Camelot?" Arthur said, looking between them.

Now Woodsmoke sighed and looked at the table.

"New Camelot?" Tom asked, confused. "Where's that?"

"Ceridwen's old castle, of course," Arthur said, through a mouthful of bacon. "Merlin's coming too. We're going to clean the place up, find some servants. What do you think?" he asked, looking excited.

Tom felt his heart sink even more. Everyone was splitting up. He turned to Brenna. "Are you going back to Aeriken?"

She nodded. "I'll spend a few days at Vanishing Hall, and then I'll go." She looked at her friends around the table. "I have some decisions to make."

Tom must have looked a little lost, because Woodsmoke said, "You're welcome to stay with me, you know that. And of course Jack and Fahey will want to see you. But you don't have to make your mind up now."

Tom had that sense of doubt again. Doubt about what he was going to do with himself and his life. Everyone seemed to have a purpose, except him.

And then he realised what he did want to do.

"You're right, Woodsmoke, I need to see granddad; I've missed him," he said. "I'll come with you, spend some time with him, and then," he looked at Arthur's expectant face and laughed. "And then I'll come and live with you for a while, Arthur."

"Good choice, Tom." Woodsmoke grinned, and slapped him across the shoulder so hard it made Tom wince. "Anyway, we'd better eat up and get dressed. We have a funeral to go to."

"Whose?" Tom asked, confused again.

"Raghnall's, of course. His servant was buried yesterday."

"But surely we're not welcome." Tom looked around the table, wondering what he'd missed, and whether they might be arrested again.

Nimue had been quiet, but now she finally spoke. "We have made a deal with the Council. In order that you are always welcome here, that I can live here, and that Raghnall's memory is preserved, we have manufactured a lie. Raghnall and his servant got into a fight and killed each other. We found their dead bodies and raced to protect the city from dragons. I have agreed to stay and defend the city. Magen, partly because he hated his father, and partly because he doesn't want a long bloody war with dragons, is supporting the lie and has agreed to let me stay. So now we go to the funeral and mourn Raghnall with the rest of city."

It was a week later, and the city had almost returned to normal. The streets had been cleared of the rich purple banners hung in honour of Raghnall. The debris left after the dragon attacks had also been cleared, and only the blackened parts of the damaged buildings remained as evidence. The town was working quickly to repair and replace the missing gilding and jewels.

Tom, Arthur, Merlin, Brenna and Woodsmoke wound their way through the city to the tunnel and the gate. They had said their goodbyes to Nimue and Beansprout at the House of the Beloved, and although Tom was sad to leave Beansprout, she had looked so happy he had to feel pleased for her.

In the end, Merlin had stayed with them at Nimue's. Nimue had refused to hear of him leaving, which Tom thought was weird. He couldn't quite get his head round the nature of their relationship. She had imprisoned him in a spell which had killed him, and yet seemed sorry for it, and Merlin didn't seem to want to revenge. It was all inexplicable. When he voiced his confusion to Woodsmoke, all he said was, "Old friends do strange things, Tom. Life's like that sometimes. I wouldn't worry about it."

They travelled down the long dark tunnel, leaving Dragon's Hollow behind them, and passed through the rose-gold gate into the bright hot sunshine of the mountainside. They stood for a few seconds, dazzled and blinking, and then looked down the mountain to where the road led to the moors and streams and then the Cervini, in a rolling tide of green. Beyond them, Tom imagined the plains and Holloways and woods stretching out all the way to Aeriken, and then to the lake and Avalon. He had travelled a long way.

Arthur shouted, jolting him back into the present, and he found he was sitting alone, the others disappearing down the path ahead. Arthur turned back to look at him. "Come on Tom, new beginnings call!"

Tom laughed and nudged Midnight into a trot. Yes, new beginnings were calling. Whatever they may be.

Thank you for reading *The Silver Tower* - I'd love you to leave a review.
The third book in the series is called *The Cursed Sword*.
Read on for an excerpt.

.

THE CURSED SWORD

RISE OF THE KING
BOOK THREE

TJ GREEN

Chapter 1 The White Wolves of Inglewood

Deep in the tangled centre of Inglewood, Tom eased his horse to a stop. In the silence that followed he listened for movement – the crack of a branch, the rustle of leaves, the skitter of footfall. Thick mist oozed around him, muffling sight and sound, and he admitted to himself he'd lost the hunt.

And now something was following him.

Tom heard the low throaty growl of the wolf moments before it leapt at him. He pulled Galatine free of its scabbard and lashed out, knowing he had only seconds before the wolf ripped his throat out. He felt its hot breath and thick matted fur, and saw a flash of its wild yellow eyes, before feeling the sword cut deep into its side. It fell back into the trees, yelping.

Midnight bolted, and Tom grabbed the reins and held on, trying to calm her down. As they pounded through the wood, a branch whipped across his chest, knocking him to the ground. Midnight disappeared into the mist. Winded, Tom lay on the damp forest floor, wincing as he felt his ribs aching. He hoped Midnight hadn't gone far. Enisled was a long walk away.

He rolled to his feet and immediately froze as he again heard the low cunning rumble of the wolf, followed by a spine-tingling howl, repeated again and again as the pack arrived.

He was surrounded.

Pale yellow eyes glimmered through the mist. As the wolves crept closer, their white fur and sharp snouts inched into view, until Tom could see the whole length of their low crouching forms ready to spring at him. Now he hoped Midnight was a long way away. They would rip her to shreds, and him too if he didn't do something.

He couldn't possibly fight them all off. The nearest tree was only a few paces away. He inched backwards until he felt the rough bark pressing into his back, and then turned and scrambled upwards, grasping at small holes and irregularities in the trunk until he reached the first branch. He heard the wolves snapping and jumping for his feet, and swung himself up, higher and higher. By the time he reached a fork he could comfortably wedge himself into, his hands were scratched and bleeding, and sweat trickled down his neck.

Gripping a branch, Tom peered down. These wolves were lean, strong, and battle-scarred, and they gazed up at him with avid hunger, settling back on their haunches, preparing to wait him out. How long could he stay here? Already the chill mist was reaching into his bones.

If he could take out a couple, the rest might flee. From his precarious position, he pulled his bow round in front of him and aimed for the largest wolf in the centre of the pack. The arrow fell short. He knew he should have paid better attention to his lessons. He aimed again. This time the arrow streamed through the air, heading straight for the wolf … then it veered off, missing it completely.

A cloaked, deeply-hooded figure emerged from the mist and raised an arm towards Tom. Not knowing if the person was threatening him or protecting the wolves, Tom lifted his bow, preparing to fire. He felt a sharp tug at his waist and looked down to see Galatine moving, struggling out of its scabbard. His hand flew to the hilt and he gripped it tightly, securing it under his jacket and cloak. The figure continued to point and Galatine continued to wiggle, and Tom quickly took aim and fired at his unknown attacker who, with a quick flick of the hand, turned the arrow. It thudded into the nearest tree.

Tom was preparing to shoot again when he heard the sound of horses approaching, and voices shouting his name. The figure turned and ran, and the wolves fled too, disappearing into the trees.

Woodsmoke, Arthur, Merlin and Rek cantered into view. Tom smiled when he saw them, feeling relieved. They were all close friends now, particularly Woodsmoke and Arthur. Woodsmoke had been the first fey Tom had met, and was now a brother as much as a friend. And of course Arthur, who had been King Arthur, sitting astride his horse, looking fully in command. Tom's relationship with him changed constantly. Sometimes Arthur was a friend, sometimes a father figure, sometimes reckless, sometimes protective.

Orlas and Rek were in their stag form, the two shape-shifting fey standing as high as the horses. The pair had been a great help when it came to finding Merlin.

And of course there was Merlin himself, whom Tom could never categorise. Old, wise and powerful, he was completely changeable, his whims and fancies unpredictable. But a good friend regardless. Merlin had also shape-shifted into a stag, one of the wizard's favourite animals.

Tom shouted down, "I'm up here!"

As they halted and looked up, the stags changed into human form, Rek and Orlas's skin dappled in browns and creams, like deer markings.

"What you doing up there, Tom?" Rek called.

"Escaping from wolves," Tom shouted to the old grey-haired Cervini, as he climbed down to join them.

"I thought maybe you were trying to turn into a bird?" Merlin said, raising his eyebrows.

Tom landed with a thump. "Funny, Merlin."

"We've been following your trail," Woodsmoke said, sliding off his horse. He looked the same age as Tom, but was in fact several hundred years older. "We saw the wolves' footprints. Are you all right?"

"I'm fine, but Midnight has bolted. She headed that way," he said, pointing into the trees. "But someone is out there, with the wolves."

"What do you mean, someone?" Arthur asked, immediately on his guard. He scanned the surrounding area.

"I don't know who – I couldn't see their face, but they had magical powers, because they could deflect my arrows. And I think they were trying to steal my sword, sort of summon it with magic."

"Show us where," Arthur said.

Tom led them to the spot where the figure had stood. "Here. As soon as you arrived, they disappeared."

Woodsmoke examined the ground. "Strange. I can't see any tracks, not even the wolves'. I can't smell anything, either."

Orlas agreed. "Nor I. But here's your arrow." The Cervinis' leader was tall and muscular, with long dark hair. He plucked the arrow from the tree and handed it back to Tom.

"I wonder who wants to hide their tracks," Merlin said, deep in thought.

Arthur shook his head. "Well there's not much we can do about it now. At least you're not hurt, Tom."

Tom grinned. "No, I'm fine. Sorry I lost you," he said referring to the hunt. "I thought I was behind you, and then I hit a thick patch of mist and the next thing, you were gone. Did you find the boar?"

"We found some boars, and killed a few, but didn't find the boar," said Arthur. "For such a huge beast, the damn thing is able to disappear pretty quickly."

Arthur had organised the hunt for the Black Boar of Inglewood, as they had named it. The forest began a few miles beyond Enisled, in a deep valley on the edge of the moors. It was dark and damp, and prone to pooling mists that hung around for days. However, it was full of wild deer, pheasants, and boar (and wolves, unfortunately) and had become Arthur's favourite hunting ground. Since moving in to Ceridwen's old castle at Enisled, he'd established some of his old routines, one of which was hunting. Slaying the Black Boar was becoming an obsession. The animal had first appeared a few weeks ago, its size making it an obvious target. But it was quick. Tom half wondered if it was enchanted.

"Anyway," continued Arthur, "the rest of the group have taken back the spoils, and we came looking for you." He held his hand out to Tom and pulled him up to sit behind him on his horse, Cafal. "Come on. We'll help you find Midnight."

They found the horse's trail, and eventually spotted her grazing a few miles on from where Tom had fallen.

A few hours later they crested a low rise, and Enisled's castle appeared in the distance. It was early evening and lights shone from the towers, the rest of the building melting into the twilight.

The castle looked very different to when they had first seen it. Then it had been sealed up, access forbidden by Herne, due to the life-giving Ceridwen's Cauldron inside. Tom and the others had been allowed to enter because Herne wanted Merlin to be resurrected.

Now that the cauldron had been destroyed by the sylphs, there was no further need for the castle to be sealed.

Up ahead, Orlas stopped to look at the view, changing to human form. "I still can't believe how different this looks, Arthur," he said, when the others drew level. "It was in a pitiful state when you bought it from me. And look at it now!"

Arthur laughed. "I have Merlin to thank for some of that. And of course the Cervini and my new employees."

"Are you really going to call it New Camelot?" Tom asked.

"Why not? I loved Camelot; it seems appropriate." Arthur seemed slightly put out that Tom should question his decision.

Merlin agreed. "It feels like home."

"But it's not very original!" Tom said.

"Isn't she beautiful?" Arthur said, gazing fondly at the castle and ignoring Tom's protests.

"Very," Woodsmoke said, rolling his eyes. He was used to Arthur extolling the virtues of his castle. "You stay and admire it, I'm heading back." He spurred Farlight on, racing across the moor, quickly followed by Rek and Orlas.

As if reminding him of the late hour, Tom's stomach rumbled. "Come on, Arthur, you're the host. No-one eats until you do. Get a move on!" And he raced away, leaving Arthur and Merlin to catch up.

As Tom strode through the door into his large second-floor bedroom, Beansprout flew from the seat in front of the fire and launched herself at him, hugging him fiercely. With the wind knocked out of him it took him a few seconds to speak.

"Beansprout!" he eventually spluttered. "Are you trying to kill me?"

"I'm just saying hello, Tom! It's been so long." She stepped back to look at him. "You've grown! And look at those shoulders! You've got all muscular, Tom."

"It's all the fighting practice Arthur and Woodsmoke make me do!" he said, feeling secretly flattered. "And it hasn't been that long – only a few months."

She smiled, and Tom couldn't help smiling back. Beansprout was his cousin, always happy and positive about everything, and she looked particularly relaxed at the moment. Her pale red hair was tied in a loose plait, and she wore a long vivid-green dress.

He gestured vaguely. "I think magic is suiting you, you look all smiley."

"It does suit me! Nimue says I'm a natural." Nimue was the priestess of Avalon who had now become the Dragon Sorcerer of Dragon's Hollow. She had replaced Raghnall, who'd been killed by Arthur and Woodsmoke after he tried to trap them in his weapons room. Without Nimue's protection spell, Dragon's Hollow would be a ruin inhabited only by dragons.

"Show us some magic, then," Tom said, curious to see what Beansprout could do.

250

"It's not a parlour trick, Tom," she said indignantly. And then she winked. "Maybe later."

"So Nimue was happy to let you leave?" Tom dropped his cloak on to the floor, before sinking into a chair and pulling off his boots.

"Not really. She said it's too soon, and I should have a full year of practice before leaving, just to learn the basics. But I drove her mad asking, and in the end she said yes. I promised I wouldn't be long, but I had to come for the tournament." She grinned at her small victory, and sat in the chair opposite him.

Arthur had decided to hold a tournament in which his new friends and the local fey would compete in sword fighting, archery, knife throwing, wrestling, and horsemanship. So many wanted to take part or spectate that it had turned into a much bigger event than originally planned, and was now being held over three days. Arthur had asked friends to adjudicate, as well as compete. The competition would begin in two days' time in the castle grounds.

"By the way, Nimue says hello." Beansprout wrinkled her nose. "Tom, you stink."

"I've been hunting all day – I was nearly eaten by wolves! Of course I stink! How is Nimue?" Tom tried to sound offhand. Nimue was probably the prettiest, cleverest woman he'd ever met, and her green eyes haunted him.

"She's amazing, of course. She teaches me so much! One day maybe I'll know half of what she does." Beansprout leaned back with a sigh. And then she added, as offhand as Tom had been, "And how's Woodsmoke?"

"Woodsmoke's … you know, like Woodsmoke. All Zen, except when Arthur goes a bit control-ish." He frowned. "Did you travel on your own?"

"No! Granddad and Fahey are here too. You've got a terrible memory, Tom."

"Oh, yeah," Tom said, as comprehension slowly dawned. "So they made it to Dragon's Hollow, then?"

"And loved it! They loved Nimue too." She smirked. "I think it's because she just let them get on with things. Unlike Fahey's sister …"

Tom looked puzzled. "Fahey's sister? Who's that?"

"Driselda. Apparently she's been living with another sister for years, but they had an argument and she arrived just after you left with Woodsmoke, with her two daughters and three sons. I think. If I'm honest, I lost track," she said, looking sheepish. "In the space of one week she succeeded in turning their routine upside down." She giggled. "It sounds quite funny really."

Tom laughed. "I bet they didn't think so. So they've moved out?"

"Sort of. It coincided with their trip, but I think they're going to see how much they like living here."

Tom looked surprised. "Here? Jack and Fahey might move in?"

"Why, will they cramp your style, Tom?" Beansprout asked with silky sarcasm.

"No! Yes, maybe." At least the castle had lots of room. As much as he loved his grandfather, he wasn't sure he wanted to live with him all the time.

"Arthur wouldn't mind, surely. He has to put up with you," she said, grinning.

"Funny." And then he had a thought. "I presume you didn't encounter any dragons on the way?"

"No! Nimue has things well under control. You should come and visit – I'll be heading straight back after the tournament."

"Maybe, but I feel like I've only just got here." He was enjoying living in the Other and didn't want to go home, but every now and again he wondered what on earth he was doing, and now he just wanted to stay at Arthur's for a while.

"Anyway, Tom, I'm starving and you stink, remember? Get in that bath or no-one will speak to you all night."

Enjoy this sample? The Cursed Sword is available to buy now.

Want to join my readers' group? Join at tjgreen.nz.

Or join my Facebook Group called TJ's Inner Circle.

Authors Note

I really enjoyed writing this book. I wanted to explore more characters from the Arthurian myths, and who could be more interesting than Merlin and Nimue! In the myths, Nimue and Vivian are sometimes interchangeable as one character with different names, or sometimes they are two separate characters. For the purposes of my re-interpretation, I decided to have them as two characters.

If you'd like to read more about the Arthurian characters, head to my website, thgreen.nz, where you can read a few posts about the tales.

Thanks again to my lovely supportive friends and family for the valuable feedback on the first drafts. Thanks also to Sue Copsey for her invaluable editing skills, to Fiona Jadye Media for the cover design, and to Missed Period Editing who edited the second version of this book.

All authors love reviews. They're important because they help drive sales and promotions, so please leave a review on either Amazon or Goodreads – or another retailer of your choice! Your review is much appreciated.

If you'd like to read more about Tom, you can get two free short stories, Excalibur Rises and Jack's Encounter, by subscribing to my newsletter.

By staying on my mailing list you'll receive free excerpts of my new books, as well as short stories, news of giveaways, and a chance to join my launch team. I'll also be sharing information about other books in this genre you might enjoy.

Note: This book was originally released called *Twice Born* in the Tom's Arthurian Legacy series. I changed the names to better suit the genre, and changed the beginning of the book because I changed the end to *Call of the King*. If you've read the series before, I hope you like the changes. I feel the stories are better because of them.

About the Author

I write books about magic, mystery, myths and legends, and they're action packed!

My YA series, Rise of the King, is about a teen called Tom and his discovery that he is a descendant of King Arthur. It's a fun-filled clean read with a new twist on the Arthurian tales.

My new series is adult urban fantasy and is called White Haven Witches. There's magic, action, and a little bit of romance.

I've got loads of ideas for future books in both series, including spin-offs, novellas and short-stories, so if you'd like to be kept up to date, subscribe to my newsletter. You'll get free short stories, free character sheets, and other fun stuff. Interested? Subscribe at tjgreen.nz.

I was born in England, in the Black Country, but moved to New Zealand 10 years ago. England's great, but I'm over the traffic! I now live near Wellington with my partner Jase and my cats Sacha and Leia. When I'm not busy writing I read lots, indulge in gardening and shopping, and I love yoga.

Confession time! I'm a Star Trek geek - old and new - and love urban fantasy and detective shows. Secret passion - Columbo! Favourite Star Trek film is the Wrath of Khan, the original! Other top films - Predator, the original, and Aliens.

In a previous life I've been a singer in a band, and used to do some acting with a theatre company. On occasions me and a few friends make short films, which begs the question, where are the book trailers? I'm thinking on it ...

For more on me, check out a couple of my blog posts. I'm an old grunge queen, so you can read about my love of that here. For more random news, read this.

Why magic and mystery? I've always loved the weird, the wonderful and the inexplicable. Favourite stories are those of magic and mystery, set on the edges of the known, particularly tales of folklore, faerie and legend - all the narratives that try to explain our reality.

The King Arthur stories are fascinating because they sit between reality and myth. They encompass real life concerns, but also cross boundaries with the world of faerie - or the Other as I call it. There are green knights, witches, wizards, and dragons, and that's what I find particularly fascinating. They're stories that have intrigued people for generations, and like many others I'm adding my own interpretation.

And I love witches and magic, hence my second series set in beautiful Cornwall. There are witches, missing grimoires, supernatural threats, and ghosts, and as the series progresses more weird stuff happens.

Have a poke around in my blog posts and you'll find all sorts of posts about my series and my characters, and quite a few book reviews.

If you'd like to follow me on social media, you'll find me here -

Website: http://www.tjgreen.nz
Facebook: https://www.facebook.com/tjgreenauthor/
Twitter: https://twitter.com/tjay_green
Pinterest:

https://nz.pinterest.com/mount0live/my-books-and-writing/

Goodreads:
https://www.goodreads.com/author/show/15099365.T_J_Green

Instagram:
https://www.instagram.com/mountolivepublishing/

BookBub: https://www.bookbub.com/authors/tj-green

Amazon:
https://www.amazon.com/TJ-Green/e/B01D7V8LJK/

Printed in Great Britain
by Amazon

22861720R00148